Child
of the
Depression

Child
of the
Depression

by

John D. Holland

RIVERCROSS PUBLISHING, INC.
New York • Orlando

ISBN: 0-944957-65-X

Library of Congress Catalog Card Number: 96-42541

First Printing

Library of Congress Cataloging-in-Publication Data

Holland, John D., 1926-
    Child of the Depression / by John D. Holland.
      p.   cm.
    ISBN 0-944957-65-X
    I. Title.
  PS3558.034853M35   1997
  813'.54—dc20   96-42541
                                           CIP

Child
of the
Depression

CHAPTER 1

His mother was an Indian girl; his father was a big tall, red-headed westerner who was on the run and who had happened to wind up in this little town. It's in the northeastern part of Macon County, in the northeastern part of Tennessee. A little town called Red Boiling Springs, which got its name from the many springs and wells of mineral waters that were there. Just seemed to be coming up out of the ground anywhere you dug a hole: sulphur water, copper water, different colors, blue, clear and yellow.

These many different mineral waters were said to be good for anything that ails you. People came from all over to drink and bathe in this mother nature's cure-all. People came from here and there to lie around and bathe and sun. People built large hotels to house the tourists. World War I made a boom town out of Red Boiling Springs. Most of the rich, and the older people came to rest and drink. They took baths and seemed to enjoy it very much.

One day in late November 1918, a couple were walking from Lafayette towards the little boom town. The man looked back and saw a big gray horse coming in a long trot, pulling a fancy buggy, so he held out his hand for a ride. That well-dressed driver was not going to stop, so the big red-haired guy just walked out into the big gray's passway and took him by the bit and said to the driver, "I just want a ride."

With a puzzled look on his face, the driver said, "Who are you?"

Holding on to the gray horse the big red-haired man said, "I'm Jim."

7

The driver looked scared and confused; finally he sad, "O.K., if that's all you want."

The big man told the girl to get in still holding the big gray by the mouth, as if he didn't trust the driver till the girl got in. He knew that he could make it on the horse or the buggy on the run. So he got up behind in the baggage carrier. "Where you from?" asked the driver.

"Too many places," Jim replied.

"I'm a salesman," said the driver. "Hope none of my customers see my hauling this Indian girl."

"Watch your mouth," said Jim. "She's as good as we are. She's my wife and she's pregnant. That's why we need the ride. Her being Indian is the reason I wanted to get out of Lafayette. I hear they don't like colored folks in that town."

"I don't blame you for that. They've been known to hang them from that big oak tree in the courthouse yard."

"This is bad," Jim said. There was not much talk the rest of the way.

All was quiet, except the roar of the wheels of the buggy and the thunder of the big gray horse's feet. Jim began to let his mind wonder. . . . Ah, yes, too many places. Thinking back on the last several years. How he was the roustabout kind. Drifting from town to town, doing odd jobs for odd folks. Just getting by, doing what he could.

The most interesting job was his last. It was a cattle drive back in Oklahoma. Even though it only lasted a few months, he got by just fine. It was good while it lasted, and the best part about that job was he had boarded near the Indian reservation where he found his beautiful Star.

The sun hung lower in the west and the clouds began to roll in. "Looks like rain," Jim said.

"It'll be a cold one," said the driver. "I will stay in Red Boiling tonight. Where will you stay?

"Don't know," replied the big man as he looked at the beautiful black-haired girl. Finally the big horse carried them into the little boom town. The driver pulled up, held back on the lines, and said, "Wo, ho! This is far as I go."

"O.K.," said Jim. "Thank you so much," as he helped the girl down out of the buggy. As they walked away the salesman just sat and looked at them and thought Ah, she is darn pretty, and I bet the big guy is okay even if he did scare me a little. Sure hope they don't have to sleep in the rain tonight.

They slowly walked out of sight. Jim didn't want to stay around town when night fell and it was getting late.

He had to wait between steps for the girl, but he didn't seem to be disturbed or nervous. They had slept in fields and woods before but had been lucky to find shelter when it rained. They had traveled a long way but Jim never seemed to want anyone to know where they had come from. He was a man of very few words, anyway. They kept on walking until they came to a road that turned to the right. It seemed to be less public with large timber on both sides. A small clear stream on the left winded its way through the beautiful forest. The birds were softly chirping a sweet tune, and the squirrels were squeaking a good night to another day.

As Jim and Star walked they hardly made any noise, for a soft bed of dead leaves covered the ground. The two never said a word to each other, just kept on walking. As they moved on Star thought about what had happened. As a young maiden growing up with her tribe, she had dreams of one day being the proud wife of an Indian brave. He would be strong and all of the others would respect him. But when this strange white man stumbled onto her reservation a year ago, she was curious and couldn't help but be drawn to him.

Star was scared, but eager to go with Jim on that dark night he had crept into her teepee and taken her away from her family. Even though she missed her people, she was the proud Star she had always dreamed of being. No matter where she was, she would be the proud wife of her husband, Jim Holt.

Finally, they came to an opening with some small fields and some rail fences. Some were made out of palings. Jim spotted some orchard trees. He was hoping there was late fruit left. Maybe some old water pears, or some limbertwig apples, for they hadn't had anything to eat all day. The sun was already down. Jim knew they would have to get hidden in for the night soon, Star was so tired. They would just have to stop soon. It was late and Jim knew he didn't have time to search for a cave or any kind of shelter.

Just then Jim saw a house and knew he'd better not go into the orchard without asking. He didn't want to be caught as a thief. The house was a large one, built out of hewed, straight logs which looked as if they had been cut with a saw. It had a porch all across the front. It seemed as if he had seen this house in one of his dreams. It looked so strong and pleasant.

As they approached the house they saw an old lady sitting on the porch, balling beautiful threads of different colors. As they drew closer, the lady looked up and saw them. She seemed to be a little shocked, but pleased. A welcoming smile came across her frail, wrinkled face.

Suddenly Jim saw a big, brown, smutty dog with every hair turned up and his teeth shining. Jim stepped between the dog and the girl, and the lady grabbed a stick and said, "Smut, come here Smut!", and she hit the big dog and made him sit down. "That rascal's mean, especially to strangers," said the lady.

Jim said, "Howdy, ma'am. Don't mean any harm. We was just passing through and I wondered if you'd mind if I could find some fruit under your trees. We haven't had anything to eat today. This is my wife, Eva Star. I'm Jim Holt. I call her Eva Star. Her name is Little Star, but I didn't like that, so I changed it to Eva Star. Little Star was her indian name, I suppose you can see she holds true to that."

The big dog snarled and growled, looking right in Jim's eyes. The lady hit him on the head, and said, "Get under the floor! That devil is mean, mean, mean. But I don't reckon we would care." It had began to rain. "I don't think you'll find anything, it's too late for fruit," she said. "Sap, my husband, is at the barn. Go ask him. Little girl, don't just stand out there and get wet, you'll be cold and take a cold. Come on in. We have a fire inside.'' She really wanted that girl to come into her house, she looked so humble and sweet.

''If that's okay,'' said Star.

''Yes child,'' said the chubby little lady. ''You look so worn out.''

''I am,'' said Star, ''but some folks don't like Indians on their land.''

''They never have run me out yet, and I'm half Cherokee,'' replied the lady. She put the big balls of thread into a box in the corner and lit a lamp. To Star it seemed so quiet and peaceful in this big house.

''Get you a chair and get up by the fire. You look cold,'' the lady said, as she took the lamp and went to the kitchen. Star sat there by the fire, as the flames leaped at the logs on the fire. As she heard the stove door open and close she smelled the aroma of bread and meat cooking. She heard the little lady call, ''Honey, come on in here if you want to. It's warm in here by this old big stove. I get lonesome for someone to talk to way off up here in these woods. Lots of the time it's just me and ole Smut. Don't know what those men are doing so long at the barn.''

Just then the old homemade door swung open and a voice said, ''Sally is it okay for this man to sleep in the barn tonight?'' A little humpbacked man came into the kitchen. His beard was white and a few days old.

The old lady took a big pone of cornbread from the hot box, and said, ''Okay with me Sap, you're the boss. When can you whip ole Smut?''

The man looked at the girl. ''Are you with that giant of a man out on the porch?''

''Yes,'' said Star. We'll leave early in the morning. Thank you for letting us get warm.'' Her heart was as warm as her body from the kindness she had gotten from the little lady.

''Sap, did that man find anything in the orchard to eat?'' the lady asked.

''Two or three ole water pears, I think? But I didn't know he had this little girl with him. Just sit still girl,'' he said and went back to the door. "Come on in. I didn't know you had a lady with you," said the little gray-haired man.

"No, it's okay," said Jim. "We have had worse places to sleep than the barn." He was just glad to have found shelter for his wife from that cold rain.

"Oh no!" said Sap. "I won't let no pretty lady like that sleep in my barn. Damned if I do!"

Jim said, "Okay if there's something I can help you do tomorrow before we leave." Jim was in no hurry. He didn't know where they were going anyway.

"We'll talk about that in the morning. Come on in and warm up."

Jim picked up his backpack and set it down beside the fireplace. He dragged up a chair and sat his big frame down by the warm, welcome fire. "I don't want to impose on you," he said as he pulled out his knife and started to peel one of the pears. Jim called into the kitchen, "Star baby, come here." He was so hungry he could have eaten peeling, core, seed and all.

"No, no," said the old man. "Keep them to take with you when you leave. You can eat with us tonight and tomorrow you can help me cut some wood, if you like."

"That's man talk," said Jim. "I like to work and think I have paid my way. Just run into some bad luck lately."

"Sally, Sally," called Sap. "Do you have enough grub for these children?" That made Jim feel real young.

"Yes, Sap. It's almost ready," Sally replied.

So Star went back into the good-smelling kitchen. She asked, "Can I help?" Some way or another she felt so loved.

"Set four plates. Wish I had a girl like you. Lost the only one we ever had." Star didn't ask questions.

"Sap, go to the spring house and get the milk, then we'll eat," said the lady of the house.

"Go wash up and I will be right back," adding "We are Sap and Sally Jones." He came back with a bucket of milk that look so clean and cold it almost gave you a chill to look at it.

Sure is a cold rain coming down out there. It may be too bad to cut wood tomorrow.

"Hope not,' the big young man said.

They all sat down at the table and the man of the house gave thanks. Star thought of being at home with her brothers and sisters on the reservation. Jim thought he had never seen a finer meal. They had cornbread, smoked shoulder blue butter beans, potatoes, sweet milk and buttermilk, fried apples, homemade butter and red eye gravy.

Jim ate till he was ashamed. He said, "This is a God-sent blessing. I will feel so good if I can help you with something. We came into Hartsville a few days ago on a train. We have ho-boed, walked and rode everything we could for a long time and a long way. My Star is the daughter of an Apache chief and I know if he ever found out where we are he would try to take her away from me no matter how far it was, or how long it took.''

Jim went on to say, "We have eaten small animals, berries, fish, and about anything we could to survive. But we haven't had anything today. Earlier today we got an unwelcome ride with some guy in a buggy. He said he was a salesman. Didn't mean any harm, but Star was give out and that big gray horse could have pulled a dozen people. Sure was a fine animal, and we needed to get out of Lafayette. We have traveled so long and so far. I would like to stop for a while if I could find some work.''

The little man went back to the living room and threw some logs on the fire and they dragged up some old bark bottom, straight-back chairs and sat down by the fire. As they sat by the fire the little old man filled a big cob pipe with some homespun tobacco crumbs and lit it with a splinter he had lying on the mantle.

As the smell of the tobacco from the ole cob pipe filled the room Jim just looked into the fire and thought how nice and how comfortable this ole home was. So quiet and warm.

Sap broke the spell by saying, "Sonny, what kind of work do you do, or what kind of job would you want?''

"I would take any kind of work that would keep me and my Star with something to eat and a place to live. I have busted a lot of broncs and branded lots of cattle. I've handled a many of cross-tie." But Jim never mentioned where he was from.

About then Sally came through the door carrying a small coal-oil lamp and Star followed close behind her. "Sap, wish I had me a girl like this," she said. "She's just too pretty to sleep in a barn. Especially on a bad night like this."

The old lady set the lamp on an old marble topped dresser and dragged the big rocking chair over close to the light. Then she picked up the box with all the big balls of thread and something with three big needles fastened to it, and started to work with the needles and thread.

Star remembered helping her mother back on the reservation make threads and blankets, but she had never done any needle work like this.

Sap took the pipe from his mouth and said, "Do you know what moonshine is?"

"Oh yes." said Jim. "I've drank some in my time." "Comes in handy some cold days when you have to be out on an ole horse all day."

Sap said, "Sal, hand me that jug out of that bottom dresser drawer, please."

She pulled out the drawer and handed him the jug and he took the lid off. The contents were yellow as gold. Then Sap passed it over to Jim and said, "Smell that."

You didn't have to put your nose to the can. You could smell that fragrance all over the big room.

"I could use a little help making this stuff, if you want that kind of job. Take a drink if you want one."

"Too full of supper," said Jim, as he handed the can back to him.

Sally said to the girl, "Get two glasses out of the cupboard. I want a little drink, and you need one too. It will be good for your tired body." So Star got the glasses and looked at Jim and said, "Is it okay?"

Jim grinned and said, "Yes, if you don't get on an Indian warpath."

"O.K.," she smiled.

Sally said, "Pour us two, honey." Star poured both glasses full.

"My, my, no, honey, we will both be on the warpath if we drink all that. Pour one back and divide the other. It is plenty powerful," said Mrs. Jones.

Sap said, "I do need someone to help, but I can't trust very many people this day. Seems like if I help you out, I could trust you. What do you think? It's hard work at a good big whiskey still. Sometimes when you get started you have to go all day and all night."

Jim said, "Star, let me have your glass."

She gave it to him. "Ah boy, that is good stuff." Star had left only a little in the glass. "Put some more in here, if it's okay with Mr. Jones."

"Help yourself," Sap said.

Star almost filled the glass again and almost emptied it before she gave it to Jim.

"I told you not to drink too much," Jim said.

The old lady just kept on knitting and said, "Well, I believe she already has. That stuff's as mean as ole Smut, and it's so good you get too much before you know it."

By now the pretty Indian girl was no longer tired and was off to her dream world sitting in her chair. "Poor thing, it will be good for her to get a good night's rest. I'll fix her a bed down in the lower room."

Somehow she felt almost as if her daughter had come home. Tears rolled down her cheeks as she walked out of the room.

She came back and said to Jim, "Take her and put her to bed."

CHAPTER 2

Star never knew that the big man picked her up and packed her to the bed, tucked her in, and kissed her good night. Jim could hear the rain hitting the board roof while he walked slowly back to the front room, he had such a warm feeling in his heart for such good treatment for his wonderful, pregnant Star. For he loved her as much as a big man could love. Sometimes he could just cry for her. She had been through so much hardship since they had met. But Star had never once wavered or complained.

As Jim entered the large, quiet room again, the lady was still quietly working and the man had just filled his pipe again. The logs on the fire had turned to a big red bed of coals.

''Come on in,'' Sap said as he sipped on a small glass of the whiskey. ''Don't drink so much of this stuff. Can't do that and make it, too. That will get you in big trouble.''

''O.K.'' said Jim. ''I never made any of the stuff, so I may not be much help, but I don't have any choice since you have been so nice to me and my Star. When do I start?''

''We'll work together,'' said the man, as he puffed on his pipe. You'll be a lot of help with those muscles. Like I told you, it's hard work. We'll have to wait till it quits raining. Then we'll cut wood for a few days. We'll need wood to warm the house and to cook with. And we'll need a lot of wood for the still.

''There's a large cedar grove back of the house and the trees are very thick and high on the hill. I piped a large spring down to the yard. It comes out of the rocks. You'd think it would be the head of the spring but the real spring is way high on the hill. I have another pipe going down into the cedars. The water there that isn't used up goes into a cave or sink-hole. I have a good set-up, but there is always a chance of getting caught.''

By now Jim was getting warm and sleepy. The little lady put her work back into the box and drank the last of her whiskey.

Jim said, "Ma'am, if we stay a while with ya'll, is there any danger of the people getting angry with you because of my Indian wife?''

As long as Sap Jones and that old dog are around I don't worry about anything bothering me. We have a mama dog by the same breed down in the shed at the barn, ready to have puppies. If you want to settle down around hereabouts, you might want one. They make good hunting dogs and good guard dogs,'' the lady said.

"Never owned any dogs but I always like to hunt and trap,'' Jim said.

By now the gray-haired man was quiet and nodding, his pipe well-burnt out in his hand. Jim aroused himself, stretched and yawned. "Excuse me, ma'am, I think I'll go to bed,'' he said. "I want to thank you again, and I will try to repay both of you, even if I do take a chance on getting caught. I always could sleep on a rainy night. Seems like this will be a good one. Sure is coming down out there.''

When Jim started to leave the room the older man raised his head from his chair and said, "Sonny, there's a night pot under the bed. Better not go outside until that ole dog gets to know you.''

"O.K.'' Jim said. "I don't think Star will even move, anyway. Holler up as early as you like in the morning. I might oversleep, I'm so tired.'' His big body was tired, but his spirit was bubbling over.

Jim made his way to the bed in the dark. It was soft and warm and felt so good. The rain sounded like lullaby music as he lay there thinking. He just had to thank God for such warm-hearted people and all they had given him and his indian wife. He kept wandering why? Was is because the woman was part indian, or because they had lost their baby girl?

Maybe I could stay close to these people Jim thought. He wanted to stop running especially since Star was pregnant. Jim knew Star needed good food and some rest. Maybe he could find some kind of shack for them to live in, and get some day work from some other farmers as well as help Sap make moonshine. One way or another he felt so good. Never really had a home to call home, just a bunk-house or box cars and eat where he could. He never did mind roughing it. But now it was different. He had his beautiful wife to care for, and soon they would have a child that he didn't want to drag from one place to another. He had to stop and settle down some way, somewhere.

Before he knew it he was awakened by the voice of the man saying, "Get up, big boy. Time to rise and shine." Sure was a short night.

"It's not raining out there this morning, but it is cold," the little man told Jim, as he went back into the big living room. Then he filled the fireplace with big logs and sat down by the fire.

Jim shook his wife. "Star baby, time to get up." She slowly opened her eyes. "Where are we?"

"Seems like heaven," Jim said.

"I don't remember getting into this good bed," she said.

Jim just laughed and said, "I know. Get dressed and come on up."

He went back into the room where the big fire was burning. Sap relaxed by the fire with his cob pipe. Smell of a good breakfast came from the kitchen.

The little man said, "Sleep good last night?"

"Never, never, had it so good," said Jim. "Sure glad the rain has stopped. Maybe I can pay you back for some of your blessings today. Do you feed before breakfast?"

"Just the horses. Done got it done. We'll finish after we eat. Can you milk a cow?"

"Yes. I have milked a lot of them and poured it down the calves before they could get up a suck, to give them strength before they could get up and go." A boyhood memory briefly flashed in Jim's mind about when he had learned to ride and bust horses and herd cattle.

"Better get washed up. Breakfast will be ready shortly," the little man said. "Is your wife up?"

"I'll go get her," said Jim.

So he went down into the room again. Star was still snuggled under the soft, warm blanket. Jim picked her up and kissed her.

Star opened her eyes and put her arms around him and said, "I love you so much."

He replied, "I love you too, but come on. Breakfast is ready. I want you to help with the chores around here if you feel like it."

"Oh, I feel good after a night like last night. Anyone would feel good but I need to go out. I'm busting."

"You can't go out. It's still dark and that dog is still out there," Jim said. "Here's a pot. Use it, and when you're through, come on up." He went into the kitchen. The sweet smell made Jim so hungry.

The old man was just drying his face. "Come on in and wash up boy. There's a pot of hot water on the stove."

So Jim got a pan of water and began to wash his face. Then through the thick-walled door came the tall, slim, black-haired young woman, with a tender smile on her face.

Jim smiled and said, "Come on and wash that indian off your face." Mr. and Mrs. Jones welcomed her with a warm good morning and she went over and began to wash in the same pan with Jim. They kissed while they washed and she whispered, "I love you."

Star dried her face and went to the cook stove where Sally was turning some large brown pieces of meat. She said, "That smells so good," and asked if she could help.

"Put four settings on the table." She kept wondering what the lady was cooking. It smelled so good.

The old lady said, "Sap, get that box of eggs out of the store room. So Sap went to a room at the end of the kitchen and came back with a full box of eggs so pretty, pink and white.

"Ever eat smoked country ham and eggs for breakfast, young lady?" asked the older man.

"Never." she replied. "Sure smells good."

Mrs. Jones cooked a platter of eggs and put them and the big plate of ham and gravy, plus a bowl of red-eye gravy on the table. Sap had stopped by the spring house to get the milk and homemade butter, as he had come back from the barn earlier from feeding the horses.

With everything on the table, Sally said, "Let's all sit down and eat."

So they all sat down and Mr. Jones said, "Ever give thanks, Jim?"

"I have a few times for a jack rabbit and a watering hole."

"Go ahead then."

There was so much to be thankful for, but he felt so empty for words. Jim finally found a few words to say and some of them was for these two people. When he was through a tear or two fell on his plate. He felt so humble and so good and so thankful. When he said, Amen, he took a dirty rag from his pocket and brushed his eyes.

Star had never seen the big man cry. She felt as if she loved him more and more every day. Then Star looked across the table towards the couple and said, "We thank you, too."

So they all ate till they got to the dessert and the little old lady said, "Have some homemade sorghum, young lady?"

"I never ate any Ma'am."

"We make it every year," said Sal. "Seems like everything is homemade around here."

"Do you get it from trees?" asked Star. She had helped her mother make syrup and sugar from sugar trees.

"No, we make it from cane. You can grow it every year."

"Do you make the whiskey out of it too?" asked Star.

"No, we make the moonshine from corn." said Mrs. Jones.

"Mmmm good syrup," said Star.

Now everybody was filled with good food. Jim said, "O.K., it's getting light, so what is next?" He was eager to get his feet on some ground where he could feel welcome.

The old man filled his pipe with strong tobacco crumbs and stuck a splinter into the front of the stove to get it afire. He lit his pipe and sat back down. He kept puffing real hard on the pipe, trying to get it afire and going.

Then he spoke up. "We will get out in a bit. Oh, Sal, I almost forgot to tell you. Kate had some pups this morning. Don't know how many, couldn't see good by the lantern. She was mad because I tried to see."

Mrs. Jones said, "Sounds like you and your dogs wished they wasn't so mean. I know they are good, but they're dangerous."

Sap replied, "They just mind their own business. You know you would be afraid here without one of them here with you when I'm gone away from the place. Besides they keep them damn cats run off from eating the pigs and chickens.

If Smut had been here years ago, Sally Ann would still be alive. That rattlesnake wouldn't have been in the garden. He would have seen to that. If Smut goes to the barn in front of me rattling around, I don't worry about getting bit by one of the critters. Not many of the law men want to nose around much either." Sap replied with a grin on his face.

"O.K., O.K.," said the lady.

"I'll go down there after a while and get Kate out and see about the pups and see how many she's got. You guys get of the kitchen and I will clean up."

Jim said, "Please let Star help."

Star said, "Go on and get your thread and get to work. Let me do this." The outline of her body was showing through the ragged clothes. Her figure was so very pretty even though she was so poorly dressed.

"We'll do it together," said the little lady.

"I need your company. If the boys can make it, we will."

Sally was so glad to have someone in her house of her race and blood. Someone she could help, maybe.

"Let's get out, Jim," said Sap.

He got a large pail that was hanging on a post at the back of the house and they headed for the barn. As soon as the bucket rattled here come that dog that gave Jim such a non-welcome the day before. As soon as he saw there were two men he dropped his tail and began to snarl and growl.

Sap said, "Smut, Smut, shut your mouth, it's okay."

The two men went into the barn. Sap gave the pail to Jim and said, "Go to the back stall on the right and milk that cow, but first we will get her some feed."

Sap opened the door to the corn crib which was almost full of corn. He chopped up about half a bushel of corn with his little short handled axe. He put some bran in it and said, "Give this to her."

Jim went in the stall and poured the feed into the trough. He thought it was a lot of feed for one cow. He heard Sap say, "I will get the mares out and harness them and give them some water. But first I have to feed the hogs."

Jim looked at the cow and said, "Gosh, no wonder that's so much feed."

It was a big cow and Jim was a little nervous. He hadn't milked a cow in a long time. But everything was going fine. His bucket was running over and he didn't want to waste the milk. He called to Mr. Jones, saying, "It's running over!"

Smut heard the strange deep voice and plunged against the wall. Barking and raising cain! Then the big cow kicked Jim. She was turning like a winding blade and he spilled all the milk. She stomped him all over and under.

Sap came running on his little legs into the barn and opened the stall door. Jim came stumbling out. He had milk in his hair and in his pockets mixed with all the other stuff. He could hardly see. The old man was just a busting, a ha, ha'ing.

Jim just grinned and said, "I didn't get done."

He went to the spring and washed his bucket, face and hands. Then Jim went back into the stable and rubbed and talked to the cow and finally finished the job. He had handled lots of cattle, but never got such a stomping before.

Jim said, ''I need to change clothes.''

He had one more pair of old jeans. He started to the house to change his britches and here comes that old dog running right at him, jumping all over him, lapping at the milk on his clothes.

''So you are laughing at me too?''

Jim changed his clothes and went back to the spring and washed his jeans. Smut stood there just watching him. When Jim started back to the barn, Smut ran along in front of him just like he was still tickled. He beat Jim to the barn then ran back and jumped up on him, still having a ball. By then Jim was a little tickled by it all. If a little milk on him for Smut to lick was what it took to make him his friend, he was glad.

CHAPTER 3

By now, Sap had a pair of big, black Belgium mares hooked to a wagon. They were fat and slick and had a good harness on them. He had axes, sledge hammers and a six foot cross-cut saw on the wagon. The old man looked like he was over the hill for the business he was in, but he had a gleam in his eye that said he was not a quitter.

So up the hill they go. The mares were just as steady as steers as they climbed the hill by the cedar thicket. Jim could tell this team had had the best of training.

The little man said, "Tomorrow we'll work in there if we can get some wood cut for the house and there, too."

When they got to the top of the hill, they bore to the right just above the large thicket of cedars and followed a wagon trail down a long ridge. Along each side stood huge timber: red oaks, white oaks, large poplars and giant chestnut trees. Smut ran along in front of the team.

Jim was just enjoying the ride and the beautiful scenery when the old man said, "Something has hit the chestnut trees, some kind of blight. See all the dead trees? They are young chestnuts. We made lots of fence rails and palings out of the chestnuts, but the dead ones make good cooking wood."

Sap pulled the team to the left into a side trail and said, "Here's as good a place as any." So they got the saw and cut dead trees and sawed them into blocks all day long.

Jim asked, "Are we going to bust it up here?"

"No," Sap answered. "We'll haul in the cut, and put it in the wood shed, then bust it when it's raining. That way we'll get more cut. We must get some hauled today. We can haul a load in an hour.''

The old man took a large gold watch from his pocket and said, ''It's two o'clock. We'll cut some trees and not saw them up.''

Jim wondered why. He was getting tired. He had never pulled a six foot saw all day. So they cut four more long trees right beside the road and left them. 'Guess we better load up. Soon be night,'' Mr. Jones said. He spoke to the team to back up and turn around. They heard every word he said as if he had sent then to school.

The wagon had a deep bed on it and was fourteen feet long. They piled it way over full then pulled up by one of the long trees that was not sawed up and took a large log chain and tied it to the wagon.

Sap said, ''Get aboard, boy. Let's go girls!''

They moved along the trail slowly and steadily. When they came to the cedars he stopped and said, ''Unhook the tree and let it lay there. We'll cut it up tomorrow. But we will have to get more to go with that. It takes a lot of wood to burn a day and night.''

Jim unhooked the chain and took one end of the log and laid it out off the road, then he climbed back onto the wagon. They headed down the steep hill. The mares were almost sitting, raring at the tongue chains to hold the wagon load to a slow pace. But the skilled old man seemed to enjoy it all.

Soon Sap stopped the team beside a long shed. ''You can put this in the shed then bust some and carry some into the gals to cook some grub. I'll put the mares up and feed them.''

Jim was busy busting wood and just thought how lucky he was to have met these people. Mr. Jones thought he would let Kate out to get some food and run around a while, but Kate found Jim in the wood shed.

That was it! She didn't like strangers at no time! Especially when she had new pups. Kate jumped at Jim and got him by the leg, cut it bad and tore his best jeans all to pieces.

Now here comes Smut, bigger and meaner. His eyes were green and his hair was rolled to the back of his head. Jim saw a ladder standing in the corner and climbed up as far as he could get. The dogs could still reach his feet but Jim kept kicking them off. The blood was running out of his boot and down the ladder.

Mr. Jones head the noise and came running with the buggy whip and shut the door behind him. He cut the blood out of both of the dogs and kept on beating them until they sat down.

Jim said, "Don't kill them. Kate has her babies to raise."

Sap said, "Come on down and we'll settle this once and for all."

Jim climbed down and Smut started on at him again. The little man hit him on the head with the whip stock knocking him down. "Be quiet!"

Finally the dogs seemed to understand that they had better mind.

Sap told Jim to sit down and let him see how bad he was hurt. Rolling up the torn pant leg he said, "Get your boot off. Pretty nasty cut, boy. Come on inside and we'll get you fixed up. Just sit on the door step and I'll be back."

Jim was so sorry that this had happened. His best jeans were almost finished, his leg was cut bad and he thought he might be crippled. For a while Jim had thought Smut was his friend, but now he wondered if he ever would be.

A few minutes later Sap came back with a pan, some rags, a cup of salt and a quart of whiskey. "Now drink half of that." Jim drank way down on the can. "Pour the rest in the pan," Sap said.

The old man put the salt in the pan. "Sit here and bathe the cut, while I get the work done at the barn." Sap went to the porch to get the milk pail and Jim was still groaning in his pain.

Sap then went to the kitchen and got another quart. "Drink some more."

He went on back to the barn and put Kate back with her pups. He thought she might start another dog fight with the stranger. Of course, Smut would help.

Jim kept on bathing and drinking until he didn't hurt anymore. Then he got up, brought the wood into Mrs. Jones and piled it behind the cook stove.

She asked, "How bad is your leg?"

"Not too bad," Jim mumbled.

"Let's see," she said. "Lord, we'll have to fix that after supper."

"Where is Star?" asked Jim.

"She's laying down. She's got a little hangover from last night." Sal replied.

"Aha, just like an Indian," said Jim. "From what I've seen, they are all alcoholics. If they get some whiskey, they just go crazy."

"Are you hungry?" asked the little lady.

"Starved is the word," Jim replied, as he staggered out of the kitchen.

He sat down on the bedside by the girl. Then Jim softly kissed her on cheek and said, "Get up you drunken indian!"

Star opened her coal black eyes and they kissed again. He showed her his leg and explained what happened. Then the two held hands as they went back to the kitchen.

Jim went to put some wood in the stove, not paying any mind to Star. He had left a quart on the table and she got the can and took two or three slugs from it. Then Jim noticed and said, "Set it down. You can't drink that every day like water. You'll hurt your baby."

"Why will it hurt? It makes me feel good," she said with a smile.

"Jim is right," Mrs. Jones spoke up. "I'll talk to you later about it."

Supper was ready and Sap came in from the barn. "How's your leg?"

"It's okay. It's not bleeding now," answered Jim.

"Jim," Sap said, "Get two buckets and get Smut to go with you so he will know you are coming back. Get some water and then we will eat."

Jim came in and said, "Some kind of a cat is a howlin' up there on the ridge. Sounds like it could eat a horse. Don't think Smut likes him any better than I do. He's growling and all his hair is turned toward his head."

"They're called lynx," the little man said. "They're beautiful cats, but they're mean scoundrels. They go for pigs, lambs, chickens or anything else they can grab. Smut don't like 'em. One got hold of him and cut him all over one time. He almost died. But they're not all bad. Those cats keep a lot of people out of the woods around here." "Let's eat."

So everyone sat down to eat, and as they sat there at the table Jim said, "Listen at that rascal still howling. I think he's coming to the house."

"No he won't. He's just daring that old dog," said Mrs. Jones.

With supper over, Star put a white bandage on Jim's leg and everybody turned in early and went to bed. Lying in bed, Jim could still hear the big bob-tailed cat howling, wailing and fussing with old Smut, but he was soon asleep. Seemed like the comfort of the big log house would let anyone sleep.

CHAPTER 4

At three in the morning, Sap shook Jim and whispered so he wouldn't wake up anyone else.

"Get up, big man."

"What? Is something wrong?"

"No, no, just got some work to do before the sun comes up," Sap answered.

So Jim got to his feet and put on his ragged britches then slipped out of the room and went down by the fire in the living room.

"How's your dog-bitten leg?" asked the little man.

"Sore," Jim replied.

"Do you think you can work on it?"

"I've had worse, busting horses," Jim said. "What's the hurry?"

"Got to get some whiskey out of the charter log, then get it to the barn before it gets light and put it under the hay. We'll eat later," Sap explained. Jim wondered what a charter log was as he hobbled around helping the little man as best he could.

The two men got the team hitched to the wagon in total darkness and pulled it out beside a shed. Sap unlocked the door and lit a lantern. They loaded several cases of cans, then Sap got another lantern and climbed onto the wagon.

The old man picked up the lines and sucked his lips to the team and headed up the hill. Soon they stopped by the heavy growth of cedars. Of course, Smut was tagging along. They unloaded the cans from the wagon and carried them into the dense trees where Smut kept growling and snarling.

31

Sap said, "Smut, what is wrong? Guess he smells that cat. He's a little weary of them. Don't blame him a bit." Jim was still worrying about the law the old man spoke of. He lit the other lantern.

Jim noticed a big white oak log on the ground. Both ends were covered with brush. Sap went to one end of the log which was a little lower than the other end and raked back some trash then said, "Hand me some cans." Then Sap uncovered a pipe which had a valve on it. He opened the valve and started filling the cans with a gold-colored liquid.

Jim was surprised, he asked, "Where is that coming from?"

"Out of the charter log," said the little moonshiner.

"How do you get it in there?" Jim asked. Feeling a little dumb, as he watched the man at his profession.

"There's a notch sawed in the other end at the top where you can't see it. This is where I pour the whiskey in."

"What kind of ends do you have on it?" Jim asked.

"Just good dressed lumber," Sap said. "When I nail it on, I drive the first line of nails to the inside next to the hollow of the log. Then I take some of Ma Sally's yarn thread and wrap between the nails to the outside, likewise with the thread. Then I drive all the nails up tight so it won't leak. If I stay in business, we'll fix another. I have another hollow white oak back on the ridge. I fill them full of dried chestnut kindling and burn them out. Then I crawl through and clean out everything but the charcoal. Before you leave, if you are going to, I'll get you to help me cut it and fix it." It gave Jim a thrill to think he might still be around that long.

Jim stayed busy, handing cans to the shiner and putting full ones in the cases until they had filled about four hundred cans.

"I would have thought that log was just laying there rotten," said Jim. Pretty clever he thought. "What do you do with the stuff?"

"It all goes to one man in Chicago." Sap answered.

"How do you get it there?" Jim asked. He was getting interested in his job already even though it was something he didn't know anything about.

"This guy buys lumber from my brother who has a saw mill in Red Boiling Springs."

Sap went on to explain, "When we haul lumber to Westmoreland, we put long lumber on the wagon first, then a short deck on each end, whiskey in the middle. We put it in the rail cars the same way, then seal the doors and the shipment goes as lumber to Chicago. Then when the cars come back, there's plenty of cans and sugar on them. We keep the same cars rented all the time."

Now the big log was empty and all of the cases of cans were loaded. The team gently got the wagon down the hill. Soon the whiskey was all buried under the hay.

"We won't need the mares no more today. Put them in the barn and feed them. I'll get the milk buckets," Sap told Jim.

Soon the chores were done. After a good breakfast the two men went back to the thick cedar grove to start filling the log once more.

"We'll need about four days to fill it again," Jones said. "This is the last time I'll use this one. I'll take the team and pull it out, then make firewood out of it." You'll like warming by this wood. It burns good and has the best of smells."

Jim worked hard all day taking orders from his boss. When the tub under the pipe got about half full they would move it, put another under the spout, then take the first and proof it down with the cold spring water and put it into the log.

"What do you do with all this waste?" Jim asked Sap.

He was speaking of all the slop and bran from the sour mesh that was made from corn meal.

"Feed it to all them hogs that run back up in the hollers. Pays two ways, my boy."

Night soon came near and Jim was tired. The little man said, "You keep the fire going under that pot while I go down and do the chores. We'll finish this run and call it a day."

As he turned to leave, the big dog got up to follow him. He said, "Stay here, stay with Jim."

The old dog crawled over to Jim and lay his head on Jim's knee. Jim could have gone to sleep because he had been sipping the new product all day.

Suddenly Smut got to his feet, his tail between his legs, every hair turned the wrong way, growling and walking. Jim thought he was getting mad at him again, but suddenly he heard something tearing the bark off a tree nearby.

Then he heard an eerie howl that would lift your hat. Jim was glad Smut was there. The old dog was very angry and nervous. The cat seemed to be daring him.

Just then, Jim heard something running through the cedars. Jim turned stiff. He couldn't move. It was Kate. She had heard that cat and Smut growling and fussin'. Kate had come to help chase the big cat away.

Jim screamed, ''Get him! Get him!''

The dogs took his order and gave that huge feline a chase across the ridge. Soon the dogs came back to Jim, whining and wagging their tails. Jim felt some better, but still didn't know if he could trust them dogs.

Smut came over and licked him on his hand and lay his head on Jim's knee again. Jim patted Smut's head. Now Jim felt like he'd finally made friends with Smut, at least he hoped so.

Both dogs lay down by the fire and seemed to be asleep, when suddenly they sprang to their feet again and started wagging their tails. Jim was glad. He knew it was Mr. Jones.

''Well, boy, looks like you done a good job,'' he told Jim.

''Hope so. Been a long day,'' Jim said.

''Yes, making whiskey is hard work. We'll get this proofed down, get it in the log, and go eat supper.''

The next three days were about the same, smelling and tasting the brew while keeping the fire going in the furnace. That dry, chestnut wood sure keeps a hot fire going. After three days, about dark, Sap poked a stick down in the log and said, ''We'll fill'er up tomorrow. We'll pour all the trash down the cave and put out the fire. That is if we don't have any company, ha! ha!''

''That cave is a great place to get rid of evidence,'' Jim said.

"Just couldn't be a better place for the business. Guess we've got everything cleaned up for today. Let's go and get some grub, son," said the little man.

Jim sure welcomed that idea. He was tired, as usual, sleepy and half drunk. Jim thought, this little ole guy is some tough hombre.

CHAPTER 5

They all ate supper that evening. The logs were burning hot and bright in the fireplace. Jones leaned back in his chair, smoking his home-spun tobacco in his cob-pipe, while Sal did her needle work.

"What was Kate raising hell about today, maw?" Jones asked.

"Oh, I forgot to tell you, that Mr. Roy Davis rode by yesterday and today, too. He stopped and asked where you was."

"Oh, got his nose stuck out again, I guess," remarked Sap. "He's a big deal lawman. He's constable. We had it out once. What did you tell him, ma?"

"I told him I guessed you was back on the place working."

The next day started off as usual back at the still. Then about eleven o'clock Kate started raising cain again. One of the mares squealed at the barn. Mr. Jones spoke up. "Believe we've got company. Just sit quiet, Jim. Come on Smut." Jim was a little nervous, he was thinkin' to himself, us or some one is in trouble.

Sap picked up his shot gun and went up the hill then came around the road above the cedar thicket, like he was hunting. Smut had began to growl and snarl, and Jones heard the sound of hoof beats coming up the hill.

Sure enough, it was that grump, Davis, riding a big, black saddle horse. Here he come, wearing his big black hat pulled down over his face and his fancy suspenders stretched tight over his belly. Even though he was a frump of a man, kinda ragged looking, with shoulders humped over, he always tried to sit up tall and straight in the saddle, acting like a big shot. Both Smut and Jones were getting mad.

Jones hissed through his teeth and the big dog went into action. The horse started to spook and wheeled around fast. Smut nailed him by the nose and threw him down on his side. The big horse fell on the riders' leg and almost broke it. The horse got up and took off down the hill, and the dog after him.

Sap was hollering, "Smut, Smut, come here!"

Davis got up, rubbed his leg and hobbled around. He shouted, "That dang dog of yours should be killed; he could get someone hurt. He's meaner than hell fire!"

"Yeah," said Sap.

"He don't have any sense," said Davis.

By then the blood was pouring down the constable's face. One ear was cut open.

"Can you walk to the house?" asked Sap.

"Maybe," said Davis.

"By the way, where had you started anyway?" Sap asked, knowing all the time he had been snooping around.

"Just loafing around," he said.

"You mean just nosing around, don't you? If we can get your horse, you better loaf around where they don't have dogs. That dog don't have no sense," Sap said.

"Guess you're right," said Davis. "Damn near got killed. Fell on that rock and almost busted my head. Looks to me like you could control that S.O.B. better than that."

"Can't get too rough on him. He might not do his job," Sap replied, as he chuckled down inside with a smirkey grin on his face.

The big black horse ran into the barn where Sap caught him. "This is a fine horse you have."

"Thank you," Davis mumbled.

"Can you get on him?" asked Sap.

"If you'll hold him, maybe I can. He thinks he's got to be running when you get your foot in the stirrup. Guess he don't know I'm not a boy anymore." Jones held the horse as Davis proceeded to mount him, looking at the blood running down on his face and just busting to chuckle. It was a funny sight to see.

Finally Davis climbed into the saddle and Smut started barking. Sap ordered the dog to sit down and be quiet, and he did just that.

"Well, how come he's minding so well now?" Davis smirked.

"Up there he just didn't have much sense," Jones told him.

Davis got straight in the saddle and looked back up the hill questioning Sap, "By the way, did you set something a fire? I see some smoke up there."

"Well, guess it's where I tried to smoke out a squirrel. Looks like as long as your nose is, you could smell just what was burning. Been trying to get some of those damn wildcats. They've been catching a lot of my pigs," Sap explained.

"Now if you think you can ride, you better go before that old dog loses his sense again. If you come back looking for me again and don't find me at the house, better not come back on the farm. I might not be with old Smut. Could just be him and Kate."

"Oh, by the way, did you see some tramps in the last few days? Really, that is what I'm looking for," the constable said. "Some folks was a little worried about them. Said it was an Indian girl and a big red-haired man."

"No, I haven't seen any tramps, but if I do, I'll let you know," Jones told him.

He walked over to the gatepost and picked up his shotgun. "You'd better follow your long nose out of this hollow if you can ride. I can tell that old dog is getting tired of sitting there. If he loses his sense again you might be trying to get out from under your horse again."

Davis took Sap's advice and pulled up on the reins, kicked his horse in the sides and down the road they went. He never looked back. Jones mumbled to himself, "Nosey lawman. Shore is a fine horse though. Well now, better get done today and get cleaned up."

He thought Davis might bring back a bunch of his kind with him, in a day or two, so he hurried back to the cedar thicket. "Boy," he told Jim, "we've got to get through today, one way or another! Davis won't be back by himself. He'll bring a crew the next time and Smut could have more than he can handle. I hate it that the horse had to get h is nose hurt, but I thought that would take care of everything."

Jim said, "I peeped out and saw what happened. He's the meanest, good dog I ever saw. Ha!"

"Yeah. Sorta hated to do it," the little shiner said. "But I had to save our own hides."

The two men continued working hard into the night to get done. They tore the furnace down and scattered all the rock, then poured all the waste and fire coal down the cave.

"We'll get the wagon in the morning and bring these barrels back up the hollow to the hog-feeding place." The log was about full once more. "They'll never notice it."

CHAPTER 6

The next morning at breakfast Jim said to Star, "I'll help Mr. Jones a while this morning while you get your clothes washed and bundled. Then we'll be on our way, that is, if I've paid our way?" Deep down Jim was dreading leaving and hitting the trail to nowhere again.

Sap was sipping his coffee as he looked across the table and asked, "Where are you going, boy?"

"I don't know. We'll find the right place somewhere," Jim replied.

"Before you go, if you will, we'll get in the buggy and go to town."

"What for?" asked Star.

"Jim needs some new britches. Them dogs tore his best ones all to shreds, and you need a few things."

Jim spoke up, "We have been well paid." He felt embarrassed, yet he was very appreciative of the old man's kindness.

"Well, are you afraid to go to town?" asked Sap.

"Hell no," said Jim.

"Well, just so happens, my brother just might need a big boy like you at his sawmill. While we're in town we can ride out there and talk to him." Jim's heart began pounding for joy.

"Just one problem though," Jim said. "Nowhere to live."

"Oh, yes, he has a few little houses he's built from the lumber at the mill. Some of the men who work for him live in them."

Sal listened to the two men talking, then sat up straight in her chair. "Well, I wish you would stay a few days longer." Her

41

eyes filled with tears. "I was making some little booties and a little sweater for someone special who'll be along before too long."

Star got up and went over to Sally and said, "Thank you, thank you," and kissed her on the cheek. The little old lady still felt like her daughter had come home.

Jim said, "Let's get those barrels moved. It will soon be daylight."

It didn't take long to get that done.

They put one of the mares back in the barn and hitched the other to the buggy. Jim said, "I had rather not do this. You don't owe me anything."

"Son," said the little man, as he climbed aboard, "I've had hard times and had to work all my life, and enjoyed all of it until we lost our only daughter. She died from a snake bite, a rattler. We could not ever have another. Seems like Ma is going to keep that girl at the house, if she can. So maybe I can help you. Besides there is enough whiskey in that log and in the barn to buy a bunch of stuff."

"Okay," Jim agreed. "Let's go."

As they started down the road Smut ran out in front of the mare. "Going to let him go to town?" Jim asked.

"Yes, he'll tend to the buggy while we look around," Jones replied. "Bet no one will bother it! "Ha, ha!"

Soon the buggy pulled up in town and stopped. Jim couldn't believe all the people. Everyone was going about there own daily business. It was Saturday, and there were lots of kids running around in the street, playing ball and being rowdy, just having a good time. Jim wondered if his children would ever run around like this in this town, without fear even though they were half-Indian. He hoped so. He prayed so.

Sap tied the mare to the hitching rail and Smut jumped up in the seat. The two men went into the dry goods store. "Morning' Mrs. Timmons," Sap said.

"Hello, Mr. Jones," said the lady behind the counter. "What can I get you today?"

Sap said, "I need two shirts, two pairs of socks, a pair of boots and a pair of overalls."

Mrs. Timmons got down a pair of britches from the shelf that she thought was about right for the little guy.

Sap held them up to the big man and explained, "I want this stuff for this boy. Sorry, I didn't tell you."

"A boy! Ha, ha!", Mrs. Timmons giggled. "How big is his dad, if this is a boy?"

So the tall, slender, blonde clerk started over and quickly brought back everything Sap had ordered.

As she scurried about in the store Jim watched her. he thought that this was a fine looking woman. She was probably in her mid-30's. Nice and friendly, he reckoned. She was married. Jim noticed her dainty hands. She had a shiny ring on her left hand. that man was lucky, whoever he was.

His lovely Star didn't have a ring. Jim couldn't afford one. Maybe someday though. Yes, Mrs. Timmons was very pretty, but Jim thought of his Star. No woman could hold a candle to her. She was the best thing in his life and would always be the best.

Jones spoke up again, "Oh, yes, I need some calico, enough to make you two dresses, one pair of ladies button shoes, and a sweater to fit about your size."

"Okay," Mr. Jones. "Boy, I don't get many orders like this."

When she had filled all the orders Sap said, "Get me two jumpers, one for me and one for the boy."

Then the lady figured up Sap's bill, smiled and said, "Gosh, Mr. Jones, almost twenty dollars!"

Sap gave Mrs. Timmons a twenty dollar bill and she gave him twelve cents.

"Good day, ma'am," Jim said as he tipped his hat and followed Sap out the door.

It took both men to carry all the goods. They loaded the buggy, got in themselves, then headed for the mill.

CHAPTER 7

Just as they got out of the buggy, the steam popped off the boiler, almost scaring Smut out of his mind. He ran off for a little while. The mare jumped up and down a little, but soon was okay. Smut came walking back very nervously and crawled under the buggy but almost immediately it popped off again. The dog took off again, whimpering and whining like a pup. He ran up on the hillside, stood and looked back like, ''Boy, that could kill a dog.'' He just stayed up there and seemed to be watching for the buggy to leave, or for the whole thing to blow up.

Sap and Jim walked up to the gray-haired man at the furnace who was chopping wood and firing the big black machine. He was sweating and was covered with black soot and ashes.

Sap hollered very loudly. ''Hello there!''

There was so much noise the man said, ''Let me get this bitch filled up, then I'll talk to you.''

He kept on chopping slabs and pitching them into the big furnace. Then he slammed the door and walked away, wiping sweat from his face. His hat was burned full of holes from the falling cinders. They walked out to the buggy.

He said to Sap, ''Looks like you bought out the store.''

''Not hardly, Dick.'' Sap said. ''This is Jim Holt. Jim this is Dick Jones, my brother.''

Dick said, ''Glad to meet ya, Jim.''

''Likewise,'' Jim replied, hoping all the time that the man had a job for him. Jim liked what he saw in this operation; he even liked the smell from the fresh cut saw dust and lumber.

Sap said, "Dick, this young man has been helping me work some. I told him you might need some help at the mill."

"Well, I just had a man quit yesterday. Marshall Capley cut his foot a little and he said he wouldn't be back. He was too light for the job, anyway. Need someone to help roll logs and chop wood for the boiler, to keep up the steam. It takes a pretty good man to do it."

"Where do you live?" he asked Jim.

Hating to face the facts, Jim said, "Nowhere right now."

"Ah, he was just traveling and stopped by the house the other day when it came that cold rain to ask if I would let him sleep in the barn," Sap told his brother. "Do you have a house empty at this time?" Sap asked Dick. He was hoping he could keep Jim around just so Ma Sally could keep the indian girl nearby.

"The guy that quit will be getting out of that house on the hill," Dick explained. "But whoever lives up there does my night watching. Before he goes to bed he comes down and checks for fire. This dust can easily catch afire. Son, are you tough enough?" Dick asked.

Sap spoke up, "He's as stout as a bull." He stayed with me pretty well, day and night making whiskey even with his leg half cut off!"

Dick turned to Jim, "If you want the job, you can have the house and your wood for nothing. The house is a good house with two rooms and a front porch. Your job will be nightwatch, fireman and help on the log yard. I will give you one dollar a day. My other men don't hardly get that much except the sawyer. He'll be your boss. The boiler has to be started and heating at five in the morning so you'll have steam by seven. I'll come in with you the first day or two."

In those days steam was used to power almost everything. All you needed was wood and water and you had power untold.

After all that spill from Dick, Sap looked at Jim and said, "Well, do you want the job or not?"

"Sure do. When do I start?" Jim smiled.

"I'll tell Capley to get out of that house. Maybe you can move in next Sunday week. Dick said. "By the way, do you have anything to move?"

"Just a few duds is all." Jim told him.

Dick said, "Well, you'll have to have a bed and a stove at least. I have a little step stove you can use till you can do better."

Dick turned to his brother. "You all have been working. How much did you get?"

"Done, or made. Ha, ha! Quite a bit. We filled that log again. We took a lot out before we started," the shiner told Dick. "I need to haul some lumber next week, at least four or five loads."

"Good, there's plenty to go. You can have one pair of my mules and wagon," said Dick. "We'll have to grease those log wagons, too, before we load any lumber. We've got time to do that now, don't we, Jim?" asked Sap. "We won't have to kill much time when we start loading lumber." Jim didn't want to take any more chances than he had to foolin' around with moonshine. That could get you canned good!

So they started greasing the log wagons. Big Jim just picked up a wheel off the ground and slipped it almost off the spindle so he could wipe the grease in.

Dick sighed, "Boy, he is stouter than a bull."

So they got the wagons greased. After that, Sap and Dick stood around and talked a while while Jim watched the operation at the Big Mill.

Capley moved out of the little house at the end of that week. Jim and Sap came over to put up the little step stove which was made for cooking and heating. Sap said, "I'll loan you one of the beds out of the lower room till you can do better."

Well, that just about put Jim out to housekeeping. He had a pan or two and a skillet. Sap went to the general store again, and told Mrs. Timmons to let Jim have enough stuff until he could get started working for his brother. Sap would pay the tab, and keep a record. Then Jim could pay Sap along after he got ahead a little.

Jim and Star got settled in the little house in town. Star was pleased. It was her first home since the reservation. She felt so secure, happy and blessed. Now she had her own house and a loving man she knew would take care of her.

CHAPTER 8

Work went well at the mill for Jim. He liked his job and the guys he worked with. Though the work was hard and the hours long, Jim would take lumber and dress it in the plainer. He made tables, chests and a cupboard. He'd work at home after his day's work at the mill till late at night. Time passed and Star was getting a little belly on her. Jim was eagerly waiting and longing for his first born child. It wouldn't be long now. Secretly he was hoping it would be a boy.

When it was time to haul out a load of lumber, Sap would come over. He'd have his farm wagon loaded down with corn and hay in that deep fourteen foot bed. He'd have it filled up with hay and, of course, the contents in under the bottom. He'd tie the stock around the farm wagon and let them eat while he and Jim loaded the lumber.

Smut was always on duty. Any time you had something you needed him to do he was around and handy. After everybody else had done their day's work and gone home, Jim, Sap and Dick would load lumber. They put a long layer of lumber down on the wagon first and a little short deck across the front and back. The middle space was for the whiskey. They stacked it full of cases and he would put a few layers of long lumber on top, tie it and boom it down. It was ready for the trip.

Sap would get on the wagon and drive the team in front, then he'd tie the other team behind the other wagon and carry two loads at once. He would get over to the railroad cars and get some black boys to help him load the stuff. He paid them off with whiskey. Every other day he loaded out two big wagons in the evening. The morning after he would leave the little town of many springs about five o'clock and not get back to the mill until late in the evening. Everyday he would come over on the farm wagon, and Smut would lie under the wagon while the stock ate. He seemed to be sound asleep but at any new or strange sound he was on his feet in a second, checking the surroundings.

One evening after the mill had shut down, it began to rain a cold rain. The two men had just finished setting the hole in the lumber full of cases of whiskey, when suddenly they heard the sound of hoof beats.

Sap motioned and said to Jim, "Hurry and get some long planks quick."

They quickly got it covered so it looked like a normal load of lumber.

A moment later a familiar big black horse came splashing towards them in the mud puddles. He was chomping at the bit and the sweat on his huge body steamed in the cool air. By the time the rider pulled up on his reins to stop the horse, Smut bailed out from under the wagon, raising hell and cane too! He seemed to know the horse, and you can bet the horse knew that ole dog.

The big horse stood straight up and lost his rider. The little shiner knowing that would distract the lawman, began to laugh.

Roy fell on a big slab right in a big puddle of water. His back hit right across the slab and he lay there moaning and groaning. "My back, it's broke!" he shouted.

He lay there rolling around in the puddle for a while and finally asked Jim to help him up. He got up out of the mudhole all muddy with water pouring out of his britches.

"Get my horse! I'll never come around Sap Jones or that damn dog again!" He was mad. Oh, he was mad all right.

Jim got on one of the mares and went after the big horse and helped Roy get on. The constable looked at the moonshiner and said, "I think you got something going and I think that dang dog knows it! Sometimes I believe you set him on me."

Jones trying to hide his laughter, and a bunch of hate, said, "Why, Roy, you know I wouldn't do that. Just the other day you said he didn't have no sense, and now you say he knows something.'' Ha, ha.

Jim listened and thought what a team the little man and the big dog was. That ole dog seemed to know what was right for the little shiner.

"Okay," said Davis, "Make him sit down while I get away and I'll never bother him again." But he was wishing all the time that he could use that ole dog for target practice.

"Sit down, Smut, be quiet and don't move," Sap demanded. "You're going to get that lawman killed!" as he chuckled inside.

"Hope your back gets better soon. We've got work to do and Smut's wanting to get up. See you around, Mr. Davis.''

The man got on his big horse and rode away once more. "That damn dog," he mumbled.

Soon the big wagons were loaded once more and ready for the trip again early the next morning.

Sap told Dick, "When I get the log unloaded again, I want Jim to help me cut and burn out one more charter log and get it in place, then that ought to do me."

Sap's bearded face was showing some regret and sadness. That won't be for a year," said Dick. "Jim may not like it that well around here."

"Hope so," Jim replied. "I like my job and the house. Star and I are liking it just fine, and I'd like to stay around if I could."

"Well, we hope so too," Sap told him.

Jim seemed to fit in anywhere there was hard work. He had worked hard since he was a young scrapper. He especially liked what he was doing now. Jim also liked the little town he somehow had happened to come into and most of the people he had come to know were just fine.

CHAPTER 9

In his spare time Jim hunted and trapped with boxes and falls. He'd catch anything to eat or sell the furs. He'd hunt out the creeks and around nearby for fish, frogs and turtles. For him and Star it was all good eating. Jim had cooked on campfires since he was a boy. He could take almost anything and make a tasty meal. He kept working, trapping and saving till he finally got enough stuff together to do very well in the little house. He started paying Sap back a little here and there, and he got enough ahead to buy more clothes for him and his pretty wife.

In the spring it was time for the baby. Sally agreed to help Star and be her mid-wife. When the time finally came it seemed as if Star were moaning and screaming all night long. Jim and Sap were in the other room wondering if it would ever end.

"Push, Star, Push hard!" Ma Sally kept coaching her. Push. Push some more, girl. It's almost here." Sally kept trying to ease Star's mind and pain.

After several hours of labor the baby was finally born. It was a girl. Jim and Star named her Eva Ann. She was a good-sized baby with very black hair. She looked indian, except her hair was curly like Jim's.

Jim was well-liked in the neighborhood and became an idol to a lot of the younger guys. He was very strong and could bust the worst of broncs. He worked at the mill for a long time. He worked in the sun, smoke and dust till his skin was a hard copper-tone color. His muscles bulged and seem to crowd each other.

A year and a half passed and a second child was born. The big man was on cloud nine now that he had a boy. He was proud of his whole family. Star was doing a great job as a mother; she was so happy. They named their baby boy, Jim Douglas which would always go short as Doug. He had red hair.

A well-known man named Joe Nash who ran the bank in the little town had learned of Jim Holt and his ability with livestock. One day he asked the millman about the big boy and about his work.

Jones, said, "Best man I ever had. Why do you ask?" Guessing he knew the answer.

From what I hear he's the man to take care of my horses. If you wouldn't get mad at me and take all your money out of my bank, I would like to talk to this man." said Nash.

"Okay," said Dick. "If it will help you and Jim, I'll be glad for both of you. Jim deserves better, and you put me to where I'm at, by helping me and loaning me money and getting me over the humps. I'll tell Jim to come in and see you."

The next morning Dick told Jim about his conversation and explained that the banker might give him a good deal. "Oh, by the way, he said to bring your wife and kids with you."

Jim said, "I don't know what to think? Don't I suit you anymore?"

"Sure boy, I like the banker, too. That banker carried my loan since I sawed my first plank. Till the war started and things got better," Dick went on. "Nash owns a fine farm and some of the best horses in the country. That big, black horse the lawman rides was foaled over there. In fact, I bought that pair of bay mules from him. He has draft stock, too. I gave him seventy-five dollars for them when they was two years old. Sounds like it might work out good. With the family coming on and all, getting out on the farm, the kids will learn a lot more. Plus as they grow, they can help with chores."

"When would be the best time to go over and see him?" asked Jim.

"Thursday evenings the bank is closed, but Nash will let you in, I'm sure. I'll go over with you and introduce you to him. He stays in his office most of the time after the bank is closed and sips on some of Sap's medicine before he goes home.'' The millman chuckled.

Being serious though, he said, ''Jim, I'd like to keep you, but it might be better for you to work for Nash. You think it over till tomorrow. It'll be Thursday, tomorrow and if you want to go see him, we'll go, okay?''

''Who'll fire ole Smokey while we're gone?''

''We'll shut her down. The men can haul out lumber and stack it. We're getting piled up anyway,'' Dick said.

''Okay.'' Jim agreed. ''It won't hurt to check it out,'' thinking this is what he would like. He had always loved working with livestock.

CHAPTER 10

The next day was beautiful. Not a cloud in the sky. Dick and Jim shut down the mill at noon. Dick told his other men what to do about hauling and stacking out the lumber. "Get both teams of mules out of the barn and get them hooked up. I'll use the black pair this afternoon."

Jim got Star and the babies and they got on the wagon and headed over to the bank which wasn't very far. When they got there they saw a big red mare hitched to a nice buggy, Sap's buggy was there too.

Dick laughed and said, "Yep, he's still here and my brother is too. I couldn't guess what was going on," giving Jim a curious grin. He was hoping those two hadn't gotten too much of a good thing. Ha. Ha.

Dick tied the mules to the hitch rail and went to the back door and knocked, saying, "Hey, Joe."

The bald-headed squatty man opened the door. "Come on in," he said. "Want a drink? We were just trying some of your brother's tonic."

"No, no, I've got someone out here to see you," Dick said. "I brought Jim Holt over to see you. He has his family out here waiting." Dick motioned out front.

"O.K." said the banker. "Bring him in. We were just talking about him, Sap says he's okay."

Jim came in carrying Doug and Star followed with Eva Ann in her arms. Dick went through the introductions and they all got seated. Mr. Nash asked Jim, "How do you like our town of many waters?"

"Fine." Jim answered.

"They tell me you're good with horses."

Just then the Jones brothers got up and said they had to go. Nash said, "You boys wait in the other room. I want to talk to ya'll in a while." He closed the door and got back to Jim asking a lot of questions and getting few answers.

Jim finally asked, "What did you want to see me about?"

"Well, boy, you're a man of few words. I can see that right now. I'll get to the point. I need a good man to take care of my horses and to help with the farm work. I have breeding stock. I have saddle and draft stock. I have several horses for saddle breeding and some draft mares. I have five stable stock for stud services. I hear you're pretty good breaking horses. Can you fit a shoe and nail it on like it should be? Looks like you could pack a great big horse."

"Ha," Jim laughed. "I can ride very well and don't have any trouble with shoeing."

"Well," said the banker, "you can think this over for a while. Guess them boys out there think I've forgotten them. If you think you would like it, we'll talk some more. Thanks for coming by."

Everyone stood up. "See you." said Jim.

Joe picked up his can and went in where Sap and Dick were waiting. "Boys, why didn't you tell me that man had an Indian for a wife? I don't know what people would say if I let that indian live on my farm." he said.

"Ha," laughed Dick, "no one has said a word to me about her and they have been with me for a long time. In fact, I don't give a damn. Hope you don't want him! He can work for me from now on regardless of the indian girl, and what anybody says." Dick spurted.

Sap said, "Well, Sal is Indian blood and I think she's a good gal and no one has ever bothered us."

"No wonder," remarked Joe. "Them dogs see to that!"

"Well," said Sap, "I gave Jim one of the pups. Maybe that'll help, ha ha!"

Dick went on, "He's everybody's pet. He stays at the mill most all the time. He's bigger than Smut."

Sap grinned and replied, "He should be; he eats all the scraps the boys have left from their lunches."

"I need that boy," said the banker. The banker was somewhat selfish in his thinking when there was a way to help himself and his pocket.

"Yes, he's just the man I need. I'll try to make a deal with him anyway.. Can you get him to come down to the farm on Sunday, Dick?" He went on, "I want him to see the place and look things over, you know, see where he would work and live and all."

"I'll ask him now," Dick said. A few minutes later Dick returned. "We'll be there."

Sap said, "I'll come too, if it's okay, and I'll try to remember to put a jar in the buggy." he laughed.

"Sure," said Mr. Nash. "Boys, I gotta get home now. Guess óle Bet has stood out there at that buggy long enough. See you guys Sunday, say about one o'clock."

So everybody loaded up and went home. That night Star and Jim talked about the possibility of the new job with the banker. They were both very excited and hoped it would work out. Little Eva Ann and Doug were asleep and Star and Jim soon got ready to go to bed.

Jim watched as Star slowly unbraided her long, silky hair. In the moonlight her hair looked like smooth black satin. Jim went over to his maiden and kissed her tenderly.

CHAPTER 11

On Sunday morning the three men went down the creek about four miles. Jim felt as if maybe he had found a place that he could settle down. Eventually they came to a white two-story house.

Sap said, "There it is, boy." Joe was at the barn when he heard them drive up. He called to them and waved for them to come on down to the barn.

There were fences and more fences, some made of pole and some built out of rail. They were all very high. Jim was amazed. The place seemed to be covered with horses. The barn was very noisy with squealing and the jacks were braying.

Joe said, "Well, I'll start off by showing you some of the breeding stock." Seemed as if he was half way bragging a bit.

Nash proudly brought the studs into the hallway, one at a time to show them off. He had a very long whip. When he opened the door the stud came out raring and snorting. First he let out a big Belgium. It was a dark bay. He let it run around a while then took the whip and put him back in the stall.

"That's my work horse," he replied.

Then he let out a black saddle horse; next was a big sorrel. He showed them two jacks. The men walked around to the back of the barn where the mares were eating hay. They had new foals with them.

With his hat sitting way back on his bald head, Joe asked, "Boy, do you like what you see?"

"I always like to look at good stock," Jim remarked. "I grew up with horses and cattle."

"Well," said the banker, "I will tell you the deal I have in mind. If you can bust young broncs and shoe the ole ones. I am sure you can feed, mend harnesses and fix fences, right? There's plenty of hard work to be done. One reason I am letting the man go that I've got is he's getting too old to do the job. He's getting afraid of the stable stock. They can be dangerous, you know. I'll give you thirty dollars a month and you can get your bread corn out of the crib and milk a cow for your family."

Jim was glad to hear he could have milk for the children. They would need it as they were growing up.

Nash pointed and went on, saying, "There is a three-room house right down there with a good garden. If you get caught up with your work and want to work for the man down the creek, he'll pay you to help him. His name is Pete Taylor. He does all the farming. Him and his five boys.

"Pete puts all the feed in the barn and keeps all the work stock down at the barns down there. You'll keep them shoed for him. There's two horses and six mules, plus some sheep and hogs down there. He sees to all that."

Nash kept on talking, "Your job will be around the barn, up here most of the time. On wet days the guys down the creek will help you with fencing and stuff like that, when they can't work in the crops. You can have Saturday afternoons off and and just feed on Sundays. I sell most of my young stock unbroken, but if you want to break any of them, we'll work out a deal for you to get some of the extra money. Now what do you think, Mr. Holt?"

Smiling real big, Jim said, "Sounds good enough, if there was another day or two in the week. What about nights? Can I hunt and trap around here?" he asked Nash.

"If your job is done, I could care less," the banker said. "If you think you are that much of a man, there is seven hundred acres here for you to help yourself. Wish somebody would catch these dang cats and foxes around here. They get rough on pigs and lambs."

Jim said, "When do I start to work?"

The banker lifted his hat and scratched his head a minute. Then he replied, "We'll I'll see the man in the house, you know, Cox, Charlie Cox, the man I'm letting go." "I'll see if he will agree to move out, seeing that he don't have anything done towards a garden or anything."

Then Dick said, "I'll let Cox live where Jim is now, but he may not like the two-room house, since he is so used to this house with three rooms."

"Thanks, Dick," said Joe. "It makes me feel better about asking him to move. Maybe no one will get hurt in this deal. If Jim don't let one of those horses bust his hide, ha!"

Seemed like the deal worked out good for every one but Dick, but he didn't mind too much. He liked both men and was glad to help any way he could. He thought how the banker had been so nice to him over the years and was glad to help Jim.

The Holt family gladly moved and settled nicely into their new, three-room abode, on the Nash property. Jim was pleased with his job and the neighbors and liked both. He worked hard, spending most of his time in the workshed mending harnesses, wagons and buggies. He also turned and shaped shoes for the work stock.

Winter was almost over so Jim didn't get to start trapping. Fur season was closed, but he fished the small creeks for food. He caught fish, turtles and a few frogs for a delicacy. He never seemed to get to bed before late at night, but he still got to his job early every morning.

Jim was always humming and whistling. Deep down inside he was happy. One reason was, that so far, there was no bad talk about his Indian wife. He guessed that was because he got along with some of the better business men. A lot of people worked for the millman and most of them owed the banker money. Jim knew that both men thought a lot of him.

Jim had his hands full. When spring rolled around again, it was time to put out crops and garden. Everything had to be kept in good repair and ready for service. The brood mares were foaling their colts; they had to be watched after and cared for.

Jim worked hard and enjoyed it all; sometimes he felt guilty about stealing his wife from her father and her tribe, but it was the only way to get her. The ole chief hated all white men, and that big red-haired man the most.

CHAPTER 12

Everything went along well for a few years. Jim and Star were blessed again with a third child, a girl they named Sally Star. Jim and Star worked hard. They put up food for winter in the fall. They planted potatoes and turnips and buried cabbage in the ground. They dried apples, peaches, pumpkin, and green beans.

They had almost everything that was good to eat. The kids were growing, helping and learning. At night, when fall came and there was frost on the pumpkin Jim would take Doug on his back, get the big dog and head for the woods, hunting and setting traps for furs as well as for meat. Doug soon learned all about it from his dad. Sometimes he was a little nervous when the cats got too close. He could hear them howling and squealing. Such an awful sound.

Sometimes Jim would put ole Bet to the buggy and take the family to visit Sap and Sally. They seemed like parents to the Holt family. Even Smut and Kate would welcome them, but they were getting old. One time Kate was going to have more pups and Sap told Doug, ''You can have the choice pick of the litter, son.'' That made Doug grin from ear to ear. Some way Sap felt like Doug was the grandson he didn't have, and never would.

Well, Kate only had one pup, a female. It was near Christmas so Sap brought the pup over and gave it to Doug. She was black and tan—a beauty. He called her Jip. Jim's big dog was called Gris. He and the pup soon became friends. The two dogs would play till Gris got tired and bit her a little too much. That would make Jip stop pulling his ears.

One day the banker made Jim an offer. "I've got thirty-five acres across the creek over yonder," he said. "I had to take up a note." He went on to say, "If you could manage to pay me a little down on it, I'll let you have it just for the note."

Jim asked, "How much is the note?"

Nash answered, "Four hundred dollars. The old man never could pay me nothing on it. In fact, I loaned him fifty dollars extra to try to fix some things on it. There's a fine spring there at the house. It's got some pretty good fields. Small fields and good timber."

Jim said, "I'll look at it on the weekend." So Jim and Doug went and looked at it. The house only had two rooms but it was in good shape. There was some sleeping space up in the attic. The spring was one of the best, coming out of the bluff just above the little house. Jim liked it very much and didn't see where he could lose, even if he couldn't pay for it.

So the next time Jim saw the banker he told him he'd take the property if he'd take fifty dollars down. That suited the banker to let Jim have it for fifty dollars. It looked like it wasn't worth much anyway. So they made the deeds and Jim gave him the fifty dollars. Jim went over every chance he got on Saturday afternoons and Sundays and worked, trying to fix up the ole place.

Star and the girls would go with him sometimes and help. Eva Ann and Sally Star would play in the woods and at the spring making lots of childhood memories. Jim got out good oak logs and carried them to the mill to have them sawed, and he built two more small rooms onto it. He made boards, recovered the whole house and had it looking pretty much like a little farm home. He was real pleased with it.

By this time the girls had started to school in the little community school. The other kids in town gave them a hard time because they were half Indian, dark complected and all. But they were both real beautiful girls.

Doug had a real hard time in school and didn't want to go. Of course, back then, they didn't make kids go to school. Jim enjoyed having him around. He was getting a lot of good horse sense education, anyway, Jim believed.

Eva Ann and Sally Star were still having a real hard time. They'd come home crying a lot in the evenings after the other kids had given them a rough way to go. Star suggested to Jim one night that if there were something he could do in a business way, and not start trouble, he should do it.

Jim finally decided he ought to go to the school and talk to the teacher, a man named Phillip Watson. Watson was always well-dressed in his suit and tie. Very few men could afford a tie in their wardrobe in those days.

Mr. Watson was well-known and liked in town; he was new to the area but well-respected. He was a bachelor who looked to be in his late twenties. He had a mustache that was curled kind of funny. He probably thought it made him look very sophisticated. Actually, he was a good looking man.

Anyway, one morning Jim decided to take the girls to school. Jim met Watson at the door and introduced himself.

Jim shook Watson's hand and said, "Good mornin' Mr. Watson." Then he told the teacher how his girls came home upset and worried. His girls needed to go to school same as any kids, Jim explained. "I'm not up here to raise a whole lot of cain, but if you have any principles, you'll stop the other kids from giving my girls such a rough time.

As Jim talked Watson carefully listened and twirled his little mustache between his thumb and finger. It was a sight to behold, Jim thought. But after Jim had finished speaking, Watson assured him right away that he'd see to it that it would stop very soon. It never did seem to really stop, but Jim's visit had helped the situation.

The girls brought their books home, the few they had, second hand books they had picked up from other kids. Doug began looking through the books and he became very interested in them. Eva Ann and Sally Star sometimes sat down by the fire on a bad afternoon with Doug when he wasn't out with Jim and tell him what little they knew about the books. Doug seemed to catch on real well.

Things continued to go well. Doug grew and Jip grew. Doug, a husky, intelligent kid, learned to ride the horses. He was a good rider in fact.

Jim was real proud of his son and also proud of the girls. He was even proud of his little farm, although he hadn't paid much of it. He had worked on the house a lot. Jim began to haul rocks to veneer it with rocks. He had several piled up and had started to put a few around the little ole house. It looked like it was going to turn it into something different.

Then one day Nash said something to Jim about six young horses in the back lots. He asked, ''I don't believe you've ever broke them, have you?'' Jim told him that he hadn't, he didn't know when he'd want to bring them up there on the front.

So with dollar marks in his eyes, Nash eagerly talked. ''We'll get them up here if you want to break them. It will get you a little extra money and give me a little extra money, too. We could sell them as saddle broke.''

The banker was a shrewd operator. Anything to put a dime in his pocket, and it didn't always have to be on the up and up as long as he knew he wasn't gonna get caught.

CHAPTER 13

The next day was very hot. The sun was high in the sky and blazing down. Jim and Doug got the six young horses and drove them into the barn and around in the pound. They were gonna try to break all six.

There was one gray horse, real big and muscular, he was cross-eyed and mean. A devil in his own hide, the way he acted. Even around the other horses he was the boss.

Some way or another that horse just stirred up a weird feeling in Jim, the way he acted and everything. Jim dreaded this one a little bit, but he'd never backed down on anything and he wasn't gonna start now. He thought about telling the banker to go ahead and sell that horse unbroke, but he never had backed down on anybody. No job or any animal he'd ever seen.

So Jim and Doug left the horses there in the pound a day or two, and decided to get this horse first. Might as well get the bad one out of the way.

Finally, Jim got a rope around the big gray beast. He managed to tie him to a post on a big plank fence and he fought for a long time. Jim got a bridle on him after a while. The saddle would be next. Jim found a sturdy roping saddle. One of those expensive ones in its day. Jim knew the banker could afford one or two, easy. Because this particular kind of saddle was well built it was able to take a lot of strenuous abuse.

After a lot of maneuvering Jim managed to get a twister on the snorting devil and he got the big, western saddle on his back. Then Jim pulled the girts down as tight as he could. He believed the horse was really going to throw a big fit, so he pulled the girts again, real tight to keep him squeezed down where he couldn't draw up in a knot.

Doug watched as both the big man and the big beast still wrestled. The young boy felt his dad was a hero and believed he would eventually break and win over this outlaw.

Jim left him tied to the post while he climbed into the saddle. He thought it would give him a little bit of a chance with this horse.

This animal was mean and big and he was stout! He just seemed to be a regular outlaw for no cause at all. Jim told Doug to pull the knot in the rope and let the big gray horse go. Doug pulled the rope to let the horse free and he started rearing, squealing and bucking! Something you wouldn't hardly believe in a horse. He was so ambitious and wild.

All at once, the back saddle girt broke and that gave the animal an advantage over Jim. Jim lost his balance and went tumbling in the air over the horse's head. As he fell his chin hit the big plank fence. The horse went running around in the pound, bucking till he finally tore the saddle all to pieces and got it totally off. Jim was almost unconscious when he fell back. The big horse had broken Jim's neck. But he was still conscious.

Doug couldn't believe his eyes. It had happened so fast. He ran over to Jim and knelt down next to him. "Dad!" "Dad! Are you all right?" he screamed.

Jim softly whispered to Doug, "Doug, I never been afraid of nothing. But I was afraid of this horse a little bit. Maybe that's where I lost the battle." His eyes began to close.

"No Dad! Don't leave!" Doug cried.

He got me, and I'm gone, son. You do the best you can and take care of your mom and the girls." "You're a big boy," he gasped, "and you're tough. I know you can do it. I'm leaving everything in your hands, I love you all and we've fought a good fight. Tell mom and the girls I love'em and bye." Those were the last words that Jim ever spoke.

Doug knew his dad was gone. He could tell by Jim's stillness and his pale face that this was the tragic end. Crying and shaking and in shock, he hardly knew what to do.

Finally, he got himself together and ran all the horses out of the pound. Then he shut the gates. He didn't want them trampling his dad's body, or pawing at him.

Doug went and got help and got his father to the house and lay him on a board. Dick and Sap made a long, chestnut box for Jim from the lumber at the mill and laid him to rest in a little community cemetery nearby. That was the last of Jim Holt.

Star just couldn't believe her Jim was gone. How in the world would she go on without him? Oh, she loved him so much. How she missed him.

She remembered his rugged smile, his eyes, his gentle but strong arms around her every night. Her heart was breaking. All the town folks who knew Jim and admired him, mourned alongside the grieving Star and her young ones.

Things really got rough from then on for the widow and her three children. The banker informed them they'd have to move. He needed the house for another tenant to take Jim's place. That is, if there was anybody to take his place? But anyway, he would have to have that house.

Doug told him he would take care of the stock just like his dad did, but he was only eleven years old. The banker told him he wanted a more mature man and he'd just have to move over there on the little farm and stay a while. If he couldn't pay for it, he would have to do something else.

Nash told Doug he would let him come over and help some, to do some things and make a little money. He'd try to help him get by one way or another. Doug wasn't happy with that, but he had to move and get out of the way so the banker could get another tenant in there.

Time slowly passed. Star and the girls were still very sad and heartbroken. But there was nothing anyone could do, but weep and cry. It would just take time to heal.

Nash talked to Pete Taylor, the tenant from down the creek. He asked Taylor and two of his boys, Luke and Carl if they would help Doug and his mother gather what stuff they had and help them move and get set up in the little farm house. So that's just what they did.

It seemed like the end of the world for Doug, but he had to do the best he could. He got wood to do the cooking and warm the house. Eva Ann and Sally Star wasn't much help, they were too busy with their books anyway.

When Doug got everything done around the house he would sometimes sit around by the lamplight and work with the girls and their books. That is, after they had done their chores and picked their shoes full of cotton to have on hand. Star would make threads from the cotton and use it for her sewing. She'd take needles and the thread and make socks, sweaters and mittens for all the family.

Cotton was very much a necessity and was grown in most family vegetable gardens. It was a tradition for the children to pick the seed out of enough cotton to fill one shoe before going to bed at night.

Doug did seem to get along better with the books than his sisters. It seemed like it just fell right down his ally to figure and read and learn and spell.

They all still had a rough time. Doug would go over and help the banker with the horses. The new man, Jack Pittman, was afraid of his shadow, but Doug knew about everything. He wasn't afraid of the horses either. He did most of the handling of the stable stock because he'd helped Jim all along. Doug seemed to get along with animals as well as his dad did.

The young boy spent a lot of lonely hours after Jim died. He trapped, hunted and fished and was pretty good at it for a kid. He was glad he had learned it all from his dad especially since this seemed to be his only way to get by right now.

Doug caught food for the family to eat and in fur season he made a little money trapping and skining furs. It was real tough, but some way or another he felt like they would make it.

Often when Doug went off fishing on the upper end of the creek, he could hear the constant humming, thumping sound of

Mr. Nash's butting-ram pump. This ole pumping device was powered only by the constant stream of water pouring into it.

Oh how he wished many a time one day he, his mom, and his sisters could live in a fine house and not have to run out back to the outhouse every time the pain came! ha.

To have an indoor toilet really must be quite a luxury, he thought. Only the banker and very few others in town took this for granted.

CHAPTER 14

Months had slipped by since Jim's passing. From time to time Star headed into town to the general store. She would meet Mrs. Jones or another of her few acquaintances on the road as she walked. But her head always hung low and she rarely spoke.

Mrs. Timmons often tried to bring Star out of her shell by talking and asking about the girls, and such. But Star had little to say. She would tend to her business, get her goods from the store, and leave.

Most every night after everyone was tucked in to bed, it was hard for Doug to tell the different between his lonely mother's cry and the sound of the sad song, from the nearby whippoorwill that echoed in the darkness.

Even though Doug was the man of the house now and had to be strong, he too, missed his dad greatly and couldn't help but cry a few tears now and again when no one noticed. Doug knew he had to be strong, not only for his mother and sister's sake, but for himself too. It was a big challenge for such a young boy to lose his father right in front of him, and lost his home and everything they had all worked so hard for, with no money to speak of.

But facts was facts. Jim was gone. Doug often said to himself, if that's the way it is, that's the way it is. He had no control of what was happening, only hope for better things to come. Yes, he'd think if that's the way it is, that's the way it is.

Doug enjoyed the outdoors very much and he often took Gris and Jip out at night. The three of them would hunt the better part of the night. They would hear those big cats a squawling. It would send cold chills crawling up and down his spine. Doug's hair would stand straight up on his neck; it was an eerie feeling. But if Gris ever got one of those cats up a tree, it would jump out and get away.

Doug was sorta glad it would get away. They sounded real rough when they were howling and squawling like that and he'd heard his dad tell how they'd caught Smut a time or two and cut him up real bad. Yes, Doug was sorta glad those cats got away. He didn't want them critters to hurt his dogs, much less himself.

Mr. Nash had once said he'd give somebody a reward to catch some of the cats. They were so bad on the lambs, pigs and chickens. But it seemed like nobody could ever catch one. The banker said nobody hardly ever saw them, especially "ole howler." One of the cats seemed like it was about as big as a mule. That was one cat Doug wanted to see.

Doug remembered Nash's words, "If I could, I'd give somebody a five dollar reward to catch ole howler, and bring that cat to me."

Doug kept hunting and trapping hoping someday maybe he would get to catch one of the cats and see what it was like. Maybe get the banker's five dollars, and maybe catch more than one cat. He might make some extra money that way.

One morning Doug headed for his traps picking up a piece or two of fur as he went along. Of course, he had Gris and Jip with him. One of his traps had a poor mangy fox in it. Doug knew he wasn't any good for fur like he was, so he thought maybe he'd turn him out, let him loose and let him go. Maybe someday he'd get better maybe make a good piece of fur.

So Doug got a forked stick to let the fox out of the trap. Just as he did that here comes Gris. He grabbed that fox right by the back end and slung it around. The fox bit Doug on the ankle through his thin britches drawing a little blood.

The fox then got Gris by the nose. Gris wasn't afraid of anything, but he never touched that fox, just stood and let him run off. No sir, he didn't want to have anything to do with that fox. Jip wasn't around so, she wasn't exposed to the fox.

Doug went on running the rest of his trap line that day. Somehow or another he felt bad about the fox. It just hadn't act right. And then Gris was leery of him and wouldn't have no part of him. That bothered Doug.

He had heard of animals with rabies and it sorta got to him. He didn't know whether or not to tell his mom about what happened, but finally went ahead and told Star about the fox and how Gris had acted. Doug explained how Gris wouldn't have anything to do with the mangy thing after he saw that there was something wrong with it. Star didn't think much about it just that the boy was a little excited.

Then a few days later a neighbor down the creek reported killing a fox that had come into the yard after his dogs. They were afraid of it, so the man killed it and saw it just had three feet. He saw what kind of shape it was in, so he sent its head off to be checked for rabies. Sure enough it came back positive.

When Doug heard all that it gave him the blues pretty bad. He had no money to be treated. He just hoped that when the fox bit through his pant leg he didn't leave any of his saliva or germs in the wound. Doug worried, and his mother did too, and so did the girls for a while, but nothing happened.

Then one morning Doug got up and went outside to start to do the chores around the place and saw Gris. The dog was acting nervous. It slobbered and seemed to be very irritable. He was jumping at the other dogs and cats and what have you. It really bothered Doug.

They decided maybe that Gris had gotten rabies. They watched him for a day or two and things got worse. Gris started having fits falling down like he was dying with the fits on him. He staggered around and slobbered a lot. He still hadn't gotten into the real bad, ill, vicious stage of the disease yet. But he was getting worse and worse.

Doug put Gris in the barn. After a while the dog tried to get to Doug even through the cracks in the wall. Now there wasn't but one thing to do, and that was to put Gris out and get rid of him. He was becoming dangerous and Doug couldn't take any chance of him getting loose and escaping.

So much as he hated to, Doug took his little old single shot rifle to the barn and killed ole Gris. He seemed like one of the last friends he had. Gris sure was a good companion on his trap line and his hunting. But things had to be this way.

Doug took Gris and buried him up on the little old farm. There were tears in his eyes as he came back to the house. Star told Doug she didn't know what she'd do if the same thing was to happen to him. Doug wouldn't talk about it.

He just said, "Ah, ma, it won't ever happen to me." He didn't believe he had gotten that much of a wound from the fox, but still he was very, very sad and blue about Gris.

About a month went by. Doug would still take Jip with him and run his trap line. Then they'd go hunting at night but there seemed to be a lot missing with Gris not along. It seemed like Jip just wasn't as vicious and brave as Gris. Doug didn't enjoy it as much as he did before. Still he knew he had to do the best he could to catch food and try to make a little money from his furs, not much but enough to help buy a few things, like some clothes for the girls to wear to school. Sometimes late in the morning he'd get through with the trap line and wander back over the hills, through the large forest to the Jones' place.

Mr. Jones was most likely cutting wood or cleaning up ground or something and they'd sit down and talk about the days gone by, and how Jim Holt happened to drift into the country. Sap told Doug how he and Ma Sally gave Jim and Star shelter from the cold rain, how Jim appreciated it so much.

They talked about how the first job he had in the country was helping Mr. Jones make moonshine. Mr. Jones had just about quit big time whiskey business. He'd gotten old and really didn't need the money. He just fooled around a little now and then for his neighbors and the banker. He hardly put a lot of time into it though, but he enjoyed foolin' with it.

One day Doug was back on the farm and ran into Sap, and of course, Doug had Jip with him too. Doug told Mr. Jones about

Gris and how he had to go, how the rabid fox had been killed at the neighbors and how it had tested positive for rabies. Sap was very concerned.

Then he told Doug, ''I'll tell you boy, I know where there's a good dog the same breed as these ole dogs, and if you want, we'll go take Jip and breed her. I wouldn't mind having one of those pups, myself. Smut's still around, but he's old and worn out. He sure ain't the dog he used to be. I guess I ain't the man I used to be, either,'' Sap chuckled.

''O.K.'' Doug agreed. But he was still real down in the blues. He told Mr. Jones he'd go see the other dog sometime with him.

Doug finished his visit with Sap and wandered back into the forest. Thoughts kept running through his mind that maybe he'd go like Gris did and he thought how awful it was when Gris tore around the building when he got real far along with the rabies, trying to get to him. It hurt Doug very much to think his companion had totally gone like that.

As Doug slowly made is way towards home he could hear the sounds of the forest creatures—the crickets and frogs and the birds, also the deep hoot, hoot from the owls. Night or day he loved those sounds, but now they had lost all the sweetness and music that used to sound so good to his spirit.

When Doug got back home he tried to be cheerful but he was really down and out about it all. He could just see himself falling with the fits like Gris.

Doug wondered what would happen if he did have to go that way, but there wasn't much choice. There was no money to get himself treated and no way backwards and forwards to Nashville. He would just have to take his chances and hope for the best.

Every body was hoping that Doug's clothes had caught the saliva from that fox, and everything would be all right.

Doug made the best of it as long as he could, the best he could around his mother and sisters at least. Several more days passed and Doug still had the blues about himself and his whole situation. All that worrying had taken his sense of humor and ambition right out of him.

CHAPTER 15

One particular Saturday morn Doug took off by himself and went to check his trap lines. He had been gone all day and it was getting dusky dark. Star was beginning to worry and wander where he was. Nobody really knew where to look for the boy. Star and the girls went ahead and had their supper but now she was really getting upset, with some of the worst thoughts going through her mind.

"What will I do?" she cried. "I just can't lose Doug too! Surely he's okay," she tried to reassure herself. "Please God, let him be safe and let him come home soon," she was constantly thinking.

About 5:30, not long after supper, the girls and Selma Crabtree, an old nearby neighbor lady, decided to go looking to see if they could find Doug. Finally they saw him coming out of the woods. He was staggering, falling and vomiting.

Mrs. Crabtree yelled, "Oh, he's got the rabies! Poor Doug's got the rabies!"

Doug looked beat. His shirt was almost torn off him and his eyes were sunk back in his head. He had vomited all down his front.

Mrs. Crabtree got all excited and scared. "Oh, my Lord, what'll we do now?" Then she jumped up as far as her short, chubby legs would let her, and ran home. She got on her old crank-type telephone and put out the news. "That Doug Holt is bad off with them rabies! He's having fits just like that old dog!"

Star panicked. Eva Ann and Sally Star screamed and cried. "Doug, Doug we love you so, don't be sick. Please don't be sick like Gris."

They both ran to meet him as he came closer. Eva Ann on the left and Sally Star on the right. They tried to help him stand. They took him each by the hand and up under his shoulders to give him a little support.

When they got to the front door Sally Star cried, "Oh, mama, he stinks real bad! I think he's already about dead!"

Thanks to Mrs. Crabtree's quick gossip on the lines, the whole neighborhood knew about Doug right quick. People started coming by to see Doug out of curiosity, wanting to see somebody with rabies.

However, it turned out Doug in all his blues and misery had run into some of Mr. Jones' stillbeer back in the forest and sat down and got to sippin' on it. He began getting sick so he just decided to rest under a big tree and lost track of time. His head felt like a ton, so he closed his eyes and lay back for a while.

Doug began to think about Gris and how he missed that ole dog. While he lay there resting he also thought of his dad and remembered how they had had some good times, just the two of them, staying out late hunting out there in the wilderness.

Then Doug realized it was getting late and started home. Doug explained about the stillbeer and how he had drunk too much of it. It had made him sick and he was very sick by the time he reached the house.

Doug apologized to his mom for doing it. He was sorry he made everyone worry. Mama Star and the girls gave him some tomato juice. Then he took a good, cold bath and soon got straightened out.

All the neighbors were real happy that Doug had gotten drunk for the first time in his life.

Come morning Doug got up. Boy did he feel bad. He could barely get himself going. But he finally got up and started on his trap lines as usual. But on the edge of Doug's mind he was still leery about what might happen. He couldn't shake the miserable thoughts of the condition his companion, Gris had gotten in.

As time went on some of the folks told Doug that if he could make it ninety days, he'd probably be okay and not come down with rabies.

Finally spring arrived and his ninety days were over. Trapping season was over and Doug felt pretty good that he had escaped the tragedy.

That summer Doug helped the banker on his farm. He fished and tried to keep something on the table for his family. He and the girls also planted a garden. Nash gave Doug the empty feed sacks he had bought the horse feed in.

Doug kept on studying with the girls at night, after the usual chores and picking a shoe full of cotton. Now Eva and Sally Star had enough dresses made from the feed sacks and the thread from the cotton to get by on, to go to school.

Later on in the early fall it had gotten way down in the middle of school and there was gonna be a test and also a spelling test. Mr. Watson asked the girls if Doug wanted to come join the class. Eva Ann had mentioned before that Doug was studying and doing well without a teacher. Well, of course, Watson wanted to just see how good Doug really was.

"Maybe Doug would like to participate in the spelling bee with the other students, maybe even take the test?"

"What do you think, Eva? Will you ask Doug?" the curious teacher said, as he grinned and twisted his little mustache.

Eva Ann told Doug all about it one night but Doug was a little reluctant. He didn't mix and mingle with other boys and girls around there, anyway. But then he decided he might do it. Didn't reckon it would hurt. At least he'd have a chance to get better acquainted with some of the younger folks if he tried it.

The day finally arrived to have the Big School-to-Do. Doug, put on a pair of his better jeans and went to school with his sisters. When they got there some of the school boys pointed their fingers at Doug. "Look at our new pupil." They were trying to put him down a little bit. You could see the boys were jealous and eating their hearts out.

Doug tried to ignore them and went on and started to take the test. He did very well in arithmetic, but went all the way to the bottom in English. He also did pretty good in geography. Then came the spell down. Well Doug hung in there pretty good. He got most of them down but three or four.

The other boys who were putting him down were boiling over with envy and jealousy saying, "It's not fair, he's not a pupil!"

After it was all over, Mr. Watson commended Doug on everything and told him he'd sure like to have him as a regular pupil. Doug told Watson he didn't have time, and wasn't interested in it, either. He was doing all right like it was. He really couldn't see the need for education.

After school that day the kids were ready to go home and have a picnic the last part of the day. Then two or three of the boys came around poking at Doug again and calling him a smart-alec Indian.

They knew some of the girls admired Doug and they were jealous. After all Doug was very muscular for a kid his age and he was tall, dark and handsome. His curly hair didn't seem to fit an Indian, but he had gotten that curly hair from Jim; it was a dark, auburn color. Yes, he was a nice looking guy, and those girls went ape over him. Those boys knew it too. They had that 'get-even' look all over them. They wanted to get at Doug real bad.

So some of them pulled Doug around to the back of the school house. There were three of them. Eva and Sally Star saw that it looked like Doug was going to get into it, so they went to fetch Mr. Watson to call the boys off.

Watson said, "We'll just watch for a minute. I won't let nobody get hurt bad, but it'll be good for a couple of those boys if Doug roughed them up a little," he smirked.

The boys kept picking at Doug and pushing him around. Finally, Doug flew into the Pratt kid. He roughed him up pretty good. Then the two Carter boys decided they would help Pratt out. The three of them just about whipped Doug pretty good.

By now he had a bloody nose and a black eye. Doug never had anyone rough him up like that. He had just fun wrestled with his dad, just horse play. This was his first time for the real thing.

Finally, Watson saw it was getting out of hand and he went over and broke up the fight. Doug felt a little bit down about it since he was half indian and didn't fit in, and didn't go to school anyway. He thought maybe he'd done the wrong thing by going up there in the first place.

Watson sent young Pratt and the Carter boys on home then reassured Doug that he could come back to school when he got ready; they'd be glad to have him. Doug wiped his bloody nose on the pretty white hanky that the teacher offered and said, "Thanks, but no thanks, Mr. Watson. Me and my sisters, we'll be going now."

He never went to school again, but Doug, kept on doing the best he could, studying from the school books at home and the girls would give him all the information they had. He never seemed to give up interest in books, but yet he didn't want to go to school. After all, somebody had to work and try to make a living, and he was the man of the house now.

CHAPTER 16

Doug was still helping Mr. Nash for a little money and more feed sacks for dresses. Just so happened Nash had a certain old mare that got a hip knocked down some way or another. Doug tried to breed her to a sorrel jack and didn't know if she'd take foal or not. The banker just wanted her out of his way.

Doug's little ole farm had some grass on it. Joe told Doug, "You can take that ole mare. You can have her about making your garden. It will get her out of my way. She's no good to me."

Doug was excited to have the ole gal. She could help him drag up some wood and he could work her in the garden and who knows, she might come up with something.

He was quite thrilled on the way home and anxious to show the mare to Star and his sisters. He was smiling from ear to ear. Now they'd have a work animal to help out on the place. Doug thought he could borrow Sap's plow and hitch it to her and till a little ground up for their garden. He also got to thinking that she'd come in handy when he went hunting and trapping, especially on some of those rough trails. He could ride her instead of traveling on foot.

When he got home Eva Ann and Sally Star ran out in the yard to meet him. They were all excited. Doug kept on watching the mare as time passed and he believed she was in foal. So then he really took good care of her, hoping that she was. Eleven months ran out and she didn't have anything. Doug just about gave up.

Then one day he went back to the pasture where the old mare was eating wild grass and stuff because she didn't have anything else to eat. To his surprise he saw she had had twin sorrel mules. They were real weak and couldn't get up and down much. Being two and not one might have made the difference.

Doug was on cloud nine. He laid right in there and took care of them. He milked the ole mare and poured the milk into the colts. He finally got them on their feet. Boy they done real good. They grew up good and were beautiful colts. They were sorrel white main and tail. Doug was just on cloud nine about that. He thought he was a rich man to own them.

Nash sure was surprised. He also seemed a little bit jealous. But he had given the old mare away and couldn't really back out. She wasn't worth anything to him, but it seemed like she turned out pretty good for Doug. Star and the girls were just as pleased as Doug was.

One day Nash told Doug, "If you help the boys in the hay this fall, down the creek there, you'll have to have something for that old mare and them colts to eat. We'll have them haul you a load or two over there to keep them through the winter." That suited Doug just fine. He didn't mind the work anyway. Anything to keep them young mules growing and going.

Doug kept studying his books and working for the banker through the summer and fall. He got to doing some figuring and was very good at it.

The banker said, "Boy, if I buy you a new shirt and a pair of britches, I might let you help around the bank on Saturday, to help clean up and maybe wait on a few people. Just the smaller deals."

Boy, that threw Doug for a loop. He really didn't know if he wanted to meet the public that much or not. He didn't think he was esteemed that high either. But if that was what the banker wanted he'd sure give it a try. It seemed like the banker was all he had to rely on. So Doug went to work at the bank on Saturdays.

When the other people got a little bit behind, he'd go around and help'em out some. Nash was pleased with Doug. He trusted the kid.

Nash had a granddaughter who lived out of state. She was from Georgia. When school was out every year she'd come spend the late summer months there on the farm with her grandparents. Her name was Janie. She was a pretty kid with dark brown hair and blue eyes. She was close to Doug's age. Janie was the only grandkid the banker had.

When she visited she had a great time on the farm. Pretty much tom-boyed around. She got to watching Doug down at the barn some. The banker would be gone to work, of course, and her Grand Ma Nell would be in the big house.

Janie got to slipping down to the barn where Doug would be. She often hid and watched him around there while he did his work. She didn't want Doug to know she was around. Then Janie got to watching as Doug worked with the horses.

One day when she was hiding in the loft Doug went up there to feed some hay down and found her. Doug asked her what she was doing there. Janie tried to explain, ''I don't have anything to do at the house, so I'm just out playing around.''

Doug liked the way she looked very much but he didn't like her imposing on him like that. Also he was afraid the banker would find out and get raw about it and not let him be around anymore. Much as he hated to, he told her she'd better stay away from the barn.

''What's your name anyway?'' he asked.

''My name is Janie. I've heard my grandfather talk about Doug. You're Doug aren't you?'' she asked. ''He thinks Doug is the greatest,'' she went on.

''Yes, I'm Doug. I need to keep on working for your grandfather if I can. Seems like really the only way I got to go. Not that I wouldn't like you or anything, but you just better stay away from here,'' he warned.

Janie said, ''Well, as long as nobody knows it, it isn't gonna hurt anything. I like to watch you down here fooling with the stock. I didn't know how things like that worked. I've been hiding down here several days now just watching. I enjoyed watching you, and the stock too," she grinned. Doug was sort of embarrassed and at a loss for words.

He said, "Well, I guess as you grow older, you'll learn more about that. I learned it from my dad. I had to pick up somewhere and seems like I do pretty good with them." Doug went on to explain, "The banker trusts me with them and I don't want you jeopardizing the job I've got here. I don't make much money, but I make enough to get by on. Seems like the only way I've got to go right now. Maybe sometime or another we can spend some time together away from the barn. Maybe you could come over and visit my sisters sometime, if you don't think the banker would care?"

Janie smiled. She liked that idea very much, but she didn't know how to ask her grandpa. She said, "I don't know about grandpa, but some of these other people around here don't give Indians a very good name. I don't know whether he would or not, but some of the other people wouldn't like it, from what I've heard my grandma say."

Doug had heard enough about that already, so he said, "You go on back to the house if you got caught down here, we would both be in trouble."

Janie didn't take that too well, but she went on back to the big house. The slipping around never really stopped, but she was always careful not to get caught.

After she went back to the house Doug couldn't keep his mind off her. Doug knew he had met the girl of his dreams. If only he could muster up enough nerve to get closer to her, maybe he and Janie would start courting. Oh, but what was he thinking? What if the banker found out? No, Doug thought. He'd just have to take it slow and see what happened. Keep his distance from that spirited gal.

CHAPTER 17

Nash had promised to take Janie around the countryside as she'd always wanted to go into the caves. Janie had never been in a cave and the banker knew about a large one next to Galen. He told her they'd pack a picnic basket of food and hook ole Bet to the buggy, then go into the cave and have a day out.

Janie could hardly wait. She loved the country and she liked riding in the buggy. She had even though that Doug might go too.

Joe told Doug that the next day the bank was closed he should hook up ole Bet to the buggy. Doug could go with them just to be their company and maybe help him out with the driving.

Well, Doug though, maybe this was a good opportunity for him to get acquainted with both the banker and Janie at once. He sure did welcome the chance to be with Janie, but he wished he had some better clothes to wear.

So a few weeks later on a beautiful sunshiny morning when the bank was closed, Doug asked the banker if he wanted him to hook ole Bet to the buggy.

Nash said, "Yeah. It looks like it's going to be a good day."

So Janie and Ma Nell packed a good lunch in the picnic basket and they were set. Nash, Janie and Doug took off bright and early over around Galen. Ma Nell waved as the buggy drove out of sight.

Along the way the blue sky didn't seem to have a cloud in it. A light breeze lifted Janie's hair and tossed it to and fro. Doug was glad that he was with them. It was just a lovely day. The birds were chirping a delightful tune and there was a sweet smell of honeysuckle in the air.

When they arrived at the cave everyone got out of the buggy. Doug hitched ole Bet to a tree. Then the three of them explored quite a bit of the cave with their lanterns. The old man wasn't too much of a cave man, himself, he was trying to please the girl, but the kids wanted to keep on going. The man didn't want to go much further. They could have lantern trouble or something.

Nash didn't care for the caves too much, and the way he felt, they'd all get lost in that cave. But they kept on exploring for a while longer.

The kids were pretty well satisfied after their excursion so they made their way back outside and had their lunch. Then they all climbed back into the buggy. Nash got in first. Then Doug took Janie's hand and helped her get up in the seat. There was barely enough room on the seat for all three people, but they did fit. Doug really liked that cause he could feel his body close to Janie's as they rode along and headed back to the town of many waters.

Everyone had a real good day. Janie could see right away that Doug was a heart throb for any girl who was looking for a young guy. Tall and handsome he was. That curly auburn hair really set off all the rest of what the boy had.

She saw right away that she was sorta sliding down in lover's lane. Anyhow, they had a good day and went on back home.

When they got home Doug took the old mare back to the barn and fed her and did his other chores then started home. Seemed like deep inside something he was feeling he hadn't felt before. He kept seeing a vision of that pretty girl and feeling his heart booming up and down a little bit too much every once in a while. He had been bitten by a fox and now by a bug.

He went on home and took care of his chores, especially his pride and joy, the sorrel mules. The banker, every once in a while would say something about them. He was a little edgy because things had turned out like they had.

"You don't see many sets of twin mules, much less sorrels," he would say.

Anyhow, there wasn't a thing he could do about it because he had given that old mare to the boy. Just lucked out real good for Doug.

That same night Doug saw that Jip was in heat. So he put a lead on her the next morning and headed across the woods to Mr. Jones'. He got over there and Sap wasn't doing much so he hooked one of his mares to the buggy. Then the two of them took a ride and found the other dog Mr. Jones had been talking about, a good husky dog and good hunting dog. It was the same breed as ole Smut and Kate.

They went and got Jip bred. Doug went back home and put her up so nothing else could get to her. He didn't want anything else but that breed of dog. They had been good for everyone who had owned them. Seemed like old Smut had taken care of the little moonshiner many times.

Everything went along about normal for a while. Doug was over at the banker's, feeding and taking care of the stock as usual. He could see Janie up around the house. He'd wave to her and she'd wave back.

Doug could feel his heart, it seemed to get too big inside his body. He would often catch himself standing and gazing up that way. Then he would think about what would happen and he'd better not let the banker know what was going on, even if it was, which it wasn't.

He was getting a heart throb for Janie. The little girl seemed to feel the same way too. So she stayed away from the barn. Janie thought the banker might put a good thing to spoil if she got caught down there.

One day Doug was out in the pound and Janie came walking down through the yard. She had a little ole stick in her hand. Seemed like she was at loose ends with nothing to do. She came down to the fence and she and Doug began to talk. She told Doug how much she liked him and admired him, and how handsome he was.

Doug stood there and blushed a little. He was bashful and backward. Of course, he liked to hear the compliments, but he didn't cater to it much. He told her he'd better be around the barn doing his things. Then he told her she was pretty and he liked her, but she had better stay away from him. They didn't want things to go wrong. It would sure put Doug in jeopardy if he lost the banker.

So, things went along just about normal. Work at the barn and on Saturdays at the bank. Then the banker started having a little problem with one of his customers. Ole man Kirby owned one of the old hotels in town. It wasn't doing any good so he hadn't paid the banker anything. There was a note against the hotel and he didn't want it. It wasn't worth much. Nobody hung around no more, seemed like.

Business seemed to have slowed down with the hard times of the depression. No one hardly had any money, only a few wealthy people.

Ah, but Nash had his way of doing a little bit of underground business.

He told Doug he had a bit of a problem. He said, ''I know that ole hotel is insured. That ole man owes me twelve hundred dollars, but he hasn't got no way in the world to pay it, and I don't want that old hotel. I need you to do me a favor. I'll give you fifty dollars off of what you owe me on your farm over there if you can do it for me. Otherwise that, I might have to foreclose on you over there on your farm. You ain't in no shape to pay me nothing much no way. You might even have to move.''

That really put Doug on the spot. He didn't want to move. He didn't have anywhere to move. Doug didn't know what to do about it. He asked the banker, ''What kind of favor do you need done?''

The banker said, ''I know he's got insurance on that old building. Nobody ever is in it, hardly. It ain't making him nothing, or me either. So some night when it's coming up a thunder and lightning cloud, you just get on your ole mare and be sure it's thundering and lightning enough. You go over there and burn that old thing down. I'll collect the insurance off it and give you fifty dollars off on what you owe me on your farm.''

Well it hurt the kid to think the man would push him into a deal like this. He loved working for him. It was a living for him and his mother and sisters. There was so much to lose, it was his way of life.

He loved being on the farm with all the things it had to offer. The beauty of it, the everyday sounds and smells it were all satisfying. Even the sound of the old butting ram that sat up in the holler, thumping day and night, pumping the water high on the hill into a large tank to fall by gravity back into the home and down to the barn.

That sound went on twenty four hours a day, never stopping. It had a soothing rhythm to Doug's ears. When the days were cloudy and grey its music seemed to be louder and sweeter. Doug loved it all too much; he wanted so much for the banker to change his mind about this dirty deal.

CHAPTER 18

Doug didn't like the idea at all. He told the banker he wouldn't do it and then began to worry about having to move.

The banker might not have moved Doug out anyway, but he made Doug believe that he would. "Ah, it won't be no harm. The insurance companies are rich. They'll just think that lightning burned the old building down. When Doug had to give into defeat he had a way of making the best of it. He would say, "If that's the way it is, that's the way it is."

So Doug finally agreed and said, "If that's what I have to do, that's what I have to do." Doug wanted to know when the banker wanted him to do it. The banker thought it over. He could hold out another year or two. He'd compound interest on it and make him a little more money. As long as the insurance was enough to pay it off, he didn't have anything to worry about.

He told Doug not to be in a hurry. He would let him know when. The banker knew he had the boy in a tough place, but didn't think he would ever squeal on him.

Time went on and Doug was beginning to feel a little better. He thought the banker had changed his mind. Course, his mules had grown up big enough for him to start fooling with. Doug was working with them a little and would get on them and ride a little. But he didn't want to ride them too much, as young as they were. He was getting them pretty well where they could be handled.

As time passed by, Jip had six puppies. Doug kept two of them and he gave Mr. Jones one and some of the neighbors got the rest of them. One of the ones he kept was a great big yellow brindle dog. He had a lot of the same nature as Smut: ambitious and gritty, and not afraid of anything. Doug named this one Rascal; the other pup's name was Gypsy.

Doug still put rocks around the house a little along as he could, like his daddy had started. He had great big piles of rock around there. Rascal was lying around there one day and Doug was busy working. He dropped a rock on the pups tail and just about cut it plumb off, about half of it.

Doug saw right quick there wasn't nothing hanging but the hide, so he had to take and cut the rest of that pups tail off. Anyway, it didn't seem to hurt Rascal that much.

The pups grew up good. Doug hunted them with Jip. They were doing real good, learning to hunt and tree. Jip had grown and was getting to be a big dog. They were doing real well and had plenty of water around there to drink as they needed it.

Doug fed them all the carcasses and things he got a hold of that the family didn't eat. They made big dogs and were very ambitious. Gritty like dogs. They loved to jump every other dog that came along for a good fight. They were tough and young and pretty bad to jump them other dogs.

Things were going along for a while and Doug was still hoping the banker had forgotten the deal he was pushing him into. He should just kick his own butt for even thinking such a thing.

If only he didn't need him so bad. He didn't want to get into anything bad, but it looked like the only chance he had to save his home. Doug didn't have anywhere to go if he lost that.

Then one day the banker said, "Doug, I'm ready for you to do that job now, if you're gonna do it for me? We've waited long enough. I've compounded his interest until it might even run a little more than the insurance on the old building. It ain't making old man Kirby nothing. I want you to get the job done soon.

"So the next time you speculate in the evening when it's coming up a thunder cloud, about dark or something, go ahead and do it," the banker ordered.

Doug had no choice. He had to do what the banker said more or less, to save his way of life for his mother and sisters. He never thought there would be any suspicion of arson.

One evening in late fall it was sorta blustery weather, with some thunder clouds around here and yonder. It was a little bit after dark so Doug decided it was the best time, especially since it looked like the storm was going to sure come a good one. It appeared to be coming out of the west. Lightning was flashing everywhere.

Maybe Doug wasn't too good at clouds? But he decided to take this chance. He felt sick inside, but Doug went and got his old mare. She only had three shoes and a half on. He didn't notice it. It was raining enough around that the ground was pretty wet and muddy.

Doug went over never thinking about the pups following. Rascal and Gypsy were right behind him. About the time he got a little fire built under the corner of the ole building the lighting was flashing real bright.

Doug was about to leave when his dogs ran into the yard of a little ole lady that lived right in front of the hotel. Rascal and Gypsy ran over there and jumped on her dog and beat him up pretty bad.

So the little lady came to the door with a broom trying to run them off. Course, there was Doug leaving. Directly, the ole hotel went up in smoke.

Some talk got out about what had happened. Folks were suspicious and wondering. That cloud never really did come on up and that lady had seen somebody riding away. Talk got out and people wondered what had really happened.

The little old lady started talking about these dogs, one real big, bob-tailed dog and another big black dog in the yard. They were beatin' her dog up.

Nobody knew anyone who had dogs like that, except Doug. But nobody thought the kid would ever do anything like setting the hotel on fire. Eventually the lawman, Mr. Davis, got in on the investigation.

Roy didn't care much about the Indian family over there, anyway. He got to looking at the horse tracks and decided to go over and check. He was eager to show off his smarts, even more to get at that kid.

Davis went over and told Doug he wanted to check on his old mare's feet. Doug still hadn't noticed that she had only three shoes and a half.

Sure enough, there was the old mare's tracks just like they'd left down by the old hotel. There was Doug's big bob-tailed dog and big black dog that the old lady saw in her yard. The old lady couldn't swear really who it was leaving with the dogs and the three shoes and a half on the old mare. This sure put Doug in a bad way, and the lawman right where he wanted to be.

"Now I will take care of this half-breed once and for all!" he grunted to himself, with a hateful grin on his fat, bearded face. So the lawman, Mr. Davis, arrested Doug and took him in for burning the old hotel. He carried him all the way over to Lafayette and put him in jail. The kid was so heartbroken. He never thought it would come to this.

Doug said, "What will I do now, what will happen to my mother and sisters? How will they get by?"

The banker felt pretty guilty about that. He knew right quick he had done wrong and done the boy wrong. So he decided to go over to Lafayette and see if he could talk them into letting the boy out on bond. Maybe he would go his bond. Everybody seemed to think because the kid was guilty, and he was an Indian, they wouldn't let him make bond.

Doug felt a little bit bad about it, about how he had been tricked into it all. He didn't want to do it to start with. He began to figure a way to get out of jail. He was going to get things straight.

So Doug stood up talking to the jailer one night when the jailer had brought him his supper. While he was talking to the jailer, Doug had a little ole knife in his pocket and some way or another he conned the jailer enough that he just held the knife blade right where the door look was supposed to slam and enter back into the hole in the lock. The jailer never did notice.

As soon as the jailer walked away, Doug pushed the door back just a little where nobody would notice it not being locked. Down into the night everything got quiet. Doug pushed the door open right easy and slipped out.

He didn't get back to Red Boiling that night. He kept traveling in the woods. He got home the next day about dinner time.

CHAPTER 19

Soon the news got out that Doug had escaped jail. Of course, Doug came back home, and of course Mr. Davis was looking for him. In the meantime, Doug had eaten something at the house and headed back into the forest.

He knew the forest pretty well and it would be hard for somebody to find him. They didn't find him that day. But the next morning, Doug was at the banker's house. The banker started to go to work and he got up in his buggy not knowing that the boy was hiding just around the corner of the barn.

Suddenly Doug just threw a rope around the ole man and tied him hard and fast to that buggy seat. He hated to do it but he had to have some way out of this.

Doug drove the ole mare back down to the barn and hitched her up then he went to the house and got Janie.

He told Janie, he said, "I've got to do something, I was tricked into this! I was bribed into it and I've got to do something. I don't mean no harm doing your grandpa this way, but it's the only way out. I wish you would go with me and help me take care of him. I don't want nothing to happen to him. I want to be good to him, but I want to stir the law people up enough to know that they got to get to the bottom of this thing."

Ma Nell was still asleep and didn't know what was going on. Doug tried to tell Janie that later Ma Nell would just think they'd gone on another picnic or something. Jane hesitated. She didn't really want to go.

Doug said, "O.K., I'll do the best I can with him."

Then Janie thought maybe she'd better go along. She saw Doug was pretty well determined. He had that ole man tied down hard and fast. The banker was pretty well shook up.

Doug told him, "I'm going to be good to you, if you'll just cooperate. We're just going back to the cave for another picnic."

Doug said, "We'll take the back roads where we won't see anybody much. Doug was dirty and tired. His clothes were torn to pieces from prowling through the woods in the darkness. He looked tired, he looked sick, and he was very nervous.

He put the buggy apron over them all and saw to it that the old man was tied with the rope good and sturdy. Then Doug went back to the very same cave. He kept the old man's arms and hands tied to his body. They went way on back inside that cave.

It was dark, cold and dirty with bat manure on everything. The echo from their voices just traveling all inside the cave.

The three of them stayed in the cave a day or two and everybody got to hunting for the banker, Janie and Doug. Nobody could figure out what had happened to the girl but some of them thought that there had been some foul play. Doug had gotten out of jail and then the old man was missing.

The cave was only about a mile from the store in the Galen community. So Doug told Janie to get in the buggy and go to the store to get them some food. The old man had a little money on him and he was getting hungry, too. So Nash gave the kids some money to get something to eat.

Doug told Janie, "I will stay here with him."

He didn't want anything to happen to him, anyway. "You go up there and get us something to eat."

The cave was pretty cool back in there and the old man was getting tired, just sitting there all tied up in them ole ropes. While Janie had gone to get the food, he said, "Boy, I guess you've out done me this time."

He went on, "I didn't really mean any harm. I just thought I needed to collect that debt. When Janie gets back, if you'll untie me, we'll go home and I'll take the blame. The bank will just have to lose the money on it. We won't collect the insurance.

We'll let ole man Kirby collect the insurance and I'll get you out of this mess.''

The banker kept on talking, ''With you being a juvenile and everything, I think I've got enough pull that I can get myself out of it, if you'll just make that deal with me son. We'll get out of this cold cave and go back home. Between me and you nothing's ever happened. I'll treat you like I always have, cause I know I was the cause of all of it anyway.''

Doug's heart was bleeding for the three of them. He said, ''Well, what about my name? I have a hard enough time getting by anyway. Who's going to clear my name with the people? Who's going to trust me anymore, to work in your bank or even be in the neighborhood?

''Please, Mr. Nash. Just think of what you have done to me and my family,'' Doug said. ''You have wealth and I have nothing but my name and my family.''

Nash assured Doug, ''I told you I'll take the blame. I will. I'll clear your name. You can keep your bank job and go ahead and work for me the way you always have. Someday you might even have a permanent job in that bank, if you'd like it.''

The banker was cold and dirty and tired. His white beard was getting pretty long and nasty. He didn't look like himself lying there in the dirt listening to the bats squealing. He sure didn't look like a banker now.

It seemed like he was really sweetening up the pot right now but Doug didn't know what to say. He wondered if the man would keep his word after he was free, Doug knew he was high tempered. He might just throw a temper fit. He didn't know what to expect from Nash.

It sure was wrong to send Janie to the store to get some food with a missing buggy in the country. Nobody could find it. Janie got some food that they could eat and headed back to the cave.

CHAPTER 20

The clerk at the store got on the crank telephone and called the sheriff out of Lafayette. She told him there was a strange girl at the store driving a mare hooked to a good buggy.

Well, that got the ball rolling. The sheriff got in touch with Mr. Davis. They began to comb the country and ask neighbors and other people what they'd seen.

It wasn't but a little while before Doug had agreed to make the deal when somebody was out in front of the cave just a hollering. It was Davis. They were going to take the boy again.

Doug thought, Well, this is the end of it.

He never would be able to break jail again. The old man had given his word so he had untied him. So, Janie, Doug and the banker all came out. They were all very dirty and worn out. Even looked like cave people as they stood in front of the cave.

The banker spoke up. "Boys," he said, "this is not what you think it is. I take all responsibility for this. Doug didn't like the idea to start with. He never would have done it. I stand behind him one-hundred percent."

The banker kept talking, "I still trust him to work in the bank and I know he wouldn't cheat anybody out of a penny! It wasn't his fault to start with. I'll just lose the money myself. I won't even let the bank lose the money. It's just a bad mistake on my part."

He went on, "The only mistake Doug made was getting caught, having them dogs with him. I am sorta glad it didn't work out. I might have made a crook out of him. Up till now I always found him just as straight as he could be. That's the way we oughta raise all our children. To be straight and be honest and work.

"The only thing I've ever found wrong with Doug at all was that he made the mistake of getting caught. Now I sorta think I'm glad of that! He hadn't hurt me in any way. Been nice to me, really; he even brought my granddaughter along to help take care of me. He didn't want anything to happen to me. He just thought it was his only way out of it."

"I know he's guilty of arson and kidnapping too, but if I have anything to do with it, there won't be any charges against him. It was my mistake. I just thought the old hotel wasn't making anybody nothing. It was just sitting there, going down to nothing. I knew Kirby never could pay me, but maybe someday, maybe he could have sold the thing to somebody."

"I don't know? It just looked like a bad situation on the bank's part. I was going to have to foreclose on it and I thought the bank didn't want that ole building. It was a bad mistake on my part, but we're going to go from here if we can."

The banker then said, "I have never had to ask favors from no one, but now I'm begging for one from both of you. Please help me this one time."

Course, Mr. Davis was a little bit hard to bargain with. He said he was gonna take that boy back to jail! He caught him to put in jail and he's aiming for him to stay in jail!

Davis spurted, "We don't need an Indian running loose in the country no way! Burning buildings and catching up all the fur and everything! No!" he said. "I'm gonna take him back to jail."

Then the banker said, "Well, I guess I can't stop you from taking him to jail, but I've offered to take full responsibility for all this out of my own pocket. I was just gonna mark it on the wall as a bad mistake on my part. From here on out, I'm gonna try to go straight, myself. I'm gonna lose that money myself out of my own pocket."

Then he said, "I'm gonna give Doug his job and depend on him like I always have. If you take him back to jail I'll do my best to see that you'll never work for the county any more! You'll lose your law job! You can count this as a bribe or whatever you want. I'm taking this on me as my mistake. I've helped you out a lot of times. We loaned you money. You couldn't get by without the bank loaning you money. I think you ought to appreciate that enough. Now I'm gonna settle this with the insurance company and the court on my own.''

"You take him back to jail and you'll be sorry! You won't ever be accommodated by the bank again, that's for sure,'' Nash said.

Then the sheriff looked at the banker and Roy and said, "You can't really blame Davis, he's just trying to enforce the law, but if Mr. Nash agrees to settle it through court and pay all the bills, we'll put the boy on probation, turn him loose and let him make a living for his family. That is, as long as he doesn't get into any trouble, it will be fine with me." I guess the sheriff thought everybody needed a chance.

Doug was pleased to hear the sheriff say these words. Now it looked like he had the banker and the sheriff both on his side. Still Mr. Davis didn't want to go this way.

The sheriff told Davis, "You mess around, you're gonna keep this boy in jail. Then his mother and sisters will have no way to get by. You're just gonna cost yourself your job and your accommodations at the bank. If Mr. Nash will settle this through court, it's fine with me. As long as it's on court paper and put the boy on probation."

Doug spoke up and said, "I will accept the probation." He didn't aim to harm anybody anyway. He never intended to get messed up like this ever again. He was very sorry this had happened. It never would happen again and he would accept probation.

After the sheriff talked to Davis, he decided to let them get in their buggy and go home. But he would be after them again if they didn't come to the courthouse and get it all straight. The banker assured him that he would, and that he'd pay all the court costs. He'd also pay the insurance on the old building out of his own pocket.

Mr. Nash was glad they let the boy go home and didn't put him back in jail. He knew if Doug was in jail he couldn't live with himself, knowing that it wasn't Doug's fault. He wouldn't be able to stand it. He couldn't sleep at night or do his job at the bank.

Star never really got into the situation. There wasn't very much she could do but beg, if it had come to that. She was very proud that the sheriff had tried to help Doug.

The banker was well off money wise and it didn't hurt him that bad. Seems like he thought more of the boy after it all happened. He had tried to use him and realized that he'd made a big mistake.

Seems like everybody came out pretty well except the banker. He took a heck of a loss, as well as a bit of a beating on his reputation and his principles. Still, being in the business like he was, it soon faded away. From then on he went straight and tried to prove to people that that's what he meant to do. He always ran a clean business and bent over backwards to help a lot of people so that it would help him in the long run. As far as anyone could tell, the bank ran along as smooth as ever.

Doug just kept doing all the things he'd been doing. He helped the banker and piddled around on his little farm, trying to make a living. His mules were growing and getting big and husky. Doug had fooled with them all along from colts up and they were pretty well broken in. He knew just how to chastise them to make them mind. He had gotten a pretty good harness on them and he was real proud. Doug took special care of his mules.

Sally Star and Eva Ann often offered to help Doug groom them but he did it himself. He kept them very well brushed and combed and they were sheared and dolled up all the time.

Doug was almost prouder though, of meeting Janie more than anything he'd ever done in his life. Every time he saw her he'd feel the heart throbs. He didn't know how to approach her really, getting something serious going. It had already been going a right smart while and both of them didn't know it.

Doug got to where he enjoyed her coming down to the fence and talking to him. The banker still hadn't caught on. Soon things were getting pretty serious. Doug and Janie got a little bolder and then one day Ma Nell got to watching them out the back window.

Well, Ma Nell told the banker that she thought maybe something was about to get started with them two kids. That sorta jerked a kink in the banker's back. He liked Doug, but Doug was Indian, and Janie was the only granddaughter he had.

Nash didn't much want things to go on that way. He thought more of her as being higher in society, maybe marrying someone like a school teacher.

So he talked to Janie. He told her he thought she should stay away from the kid and leave him alone. Janie could do better than that. Not mix her race like that. This broke Janie's heart. She cried. She told her grandfather she really cared for Doug. She proved that, because she kept slipping around to see him when she could.

Things were getting a little bit more serious than anybody thought. Even more than Janie and Doug had expected. One day the banker got onto Doug about it and told him to quit talking to Janie. If he wanted to go ahead and work for him, it was all right, but Doug was gonna have to leave Janie alone!

That broke Doug's heart too, but he thought maybe when they both got older it might still work out. He didn't know. But he did know he loved the girl. He believed she loved him too. In fact, they'd talked of love a little bit, in around about backwards way.

Doug was still awkward on things like that, but he couldn't help feeling those urges and heart throbs every time he was around Janie. He really didn't know what love was all about, but when he was with Janie it made him feel so good and when he couldn't be with her it made him feel so bad.

Sometimes he'd catch a glance of her up in the yard around that big house. Just seeing her made him feel good. But when

Janie went back to Georgia for another school year every day Doug's heart was longing and yearning for summer to come again. He felt so much hurt sometimes he just wished it would all go away.

The school years seemed so long. Doug could just imagine Janie talking to other boys at school and that would hurt him very much. Looked like there was more hurt than good. He knew that her high tempered grandpa would never condone him seeing too much of her. Doug wished some way he could get rid of these feelings and forget it all.

But Doug still felt like he had some things to be thankful for. He thought of those horrible nights in jail and was so glad that was in the past. At least he was free. He thought, I can go on with my life! But I must forget about Janie. It wouldn't work out anyway, with someone like the banker standing in the way. Doug knew that his and Janie's worlds were far apart. He just had to erase all thoughts of the girl and get rid of all the heart throbs and all the wild feelings, cause it could never be.

CHAPTER 21

Things went on for a year or two. The kids got older. Doug just kept trapping. He found a place back in the forest, a great big cave. He believed the cats were living there. He took his heavier traps and set them there in the mouth of the cave.

Two or three mornings each week he would go to his traps but there wouldn't be anything in them. He kept seeing chicken bones and feathers and lamb's wool and stuff like that lying around. He was sure cats were living in the cave. Probably a family of them. He sure would like to get a hold of "ole howler" and see what he looked like. Get the banker's money anyway.

One morning Doug saw something lying out away from the den. Sure enough, he had one of the cats in his trap. He had his little ole twenty-two rifle and he kept looking and saw three baby cats down there with this cat. They seemed to be nursing on her.

Doug thought he had gotten ole howler, but then again she had baby cats and he didn't want them to starve to death. So Doug decided he'd try to get her out of the trap.

Naturally, as he approached, the cat came to its feet as best as it could. She had a trap on two feet. How in the world would he get her out? Doug set his little ole twenty-two rifle up against a tree and scratched his head.

He got a great big, heavy, forked stick and tried to press the trap down so she could get her foot out, but that didn't work.

Doug thought, well, how was he going to do this? Maybe he could put the forked stick over the cat's neck and choke it down enough, but not kill it. If he could choke her out enough, he could get her out.

The boy still didn't know how he was going to do that without the cat scratching him all over. But he decided it was the only way. Doug couldn't ever get the trap loose from her foot, but maybe he could get her choked out.

He choked the cat down with his second forked stick and mashed and mashed while she was pulling. She finally got one foot out of the trap.

Surely this ain't ole howler? Doug thought. This cat ain't as big as I was expecting it to be. But if it is ole howler, I'm turning her loose to raise them baby cats. I don't want them to starve to death.''

Doug then thought he might fix a box in that cave and catch one of the babies. He wouldn't mind having one for a pet. Suddenly he heard something behind him.

He turned around and there really was ole howler! He was a big gray cat with yellow spots all over his body. His ears were laid back, his back was in a hump and every tooth was showing!

The big cat looked like he was ready to leap on Doug any minute. The boy was terrified. He felt as if every hair on his head was sticking straight up. He moved slowly to get to his rifle. He knew if he ever got it, he couldn't afford to miss. He thought the animal might attack at the moment he moved but he had to take that chance. He had to get to his gun.

That cat was mad! It kept growling, spitting and blowing. He was all humped into a knot with his head down low, ready to pounce. Doug was very quick with his little ole rifle. He shot that cat right between the eyes.

It came towards him a right smart. But it had lost all its life before it reached him. It went down and bowed out and gave up the ghost. Doug dragged him off up the hill and looked at him. Boy that cat was big. It weighed forty-five pounds or more. But it was a beautiful animal. It had yellow eyes, a little short tail and long pointed ears with about an inch or two of hair. A little narrow, hairy bristle stuck up out of his ears.

Doug thought, well, at least I've got ole howler this time. He thought if he could pack him back to the house he'd get him over to the banker and get that five dollars. But he still had to get the mama cat out of the trap. By now, she was getting more and more angry and very vicious, which was to be expected.

So Doug went down and wrestled with her again, trying not to get cut up by her. He took his long, forked stick and choked her down so she could hardly move. Finally he got her other foot out of the trap and got back out of her way. For a moment she didn't know she was free.

Doug quickly reloaded his gun. He thought he might have to get rid of her too. Doug slipped up off behind a tree and she wiggled around and realized she was out of the trap. She galloped off down through the forest. Doug was glad he didn't have to kill her.

With the cat out of sight, Doug took a bunch of rocks and stopped up the den good and went to the house. He nailed him a box together and put him a drop lid on it then went and got some food scraps for the box.

He went back and set the trap and boxed all around it with rocks where nothing could get in or out of the den. He kept checking it for two or three days but never saw any of the kittens in it. He made sure to keep checking the surroundings while he was in the forest cause he didn't want another big cat to slip up on him again.

One morning Doug went back and saw that his trip lid had fallen. It had wire across the back and where it would look like it was daylight all the way through it where they would come near trying to go through it and get out. Sure enough, he had one of the cats. It weighed maybe two pounds, enough weight to be mean as heck, ah, but it was cute.

Doug didn't know how he was going to get that cat out of there without gettin' eaten up by him. He didn't want to have to drag the box back to the house with the little cat in it. So he quickly went back to the house and got a sack. Then he came back and cut his wire on the back of his box and stretched the sack over the end of it. Then Doug made some noise and the little thing ran right into the bag.

Doug opened the bag and looked down. He was a beauty. Almost all black with gold spots. He wasn't real black, just a real dark gray. He was a beautiful kitten.

Doug thought, well, well, if I can ever tame this cat, he'll make me a wonderful pet. Doug left the den undone so the mama cat could get back to her other kittens. He took this cat on to the house. Doug built a little cage, put a wire front on it and sat the kitten down in it. He began to pet him and feed him fresh carcasses and scraps and things.

That kitten made a wonderful pet. Just the same as a house cat, and he grew, really did grow. It wasn't long till he was half as big as ole howler.

Anyhow, Doug had taken ole howler over to the banker. The banker was surprised to see how big a cat he was. No wonder it took so many lambs and chickens to feed them, if they were all that big and had many families in the country. Nash gave Doug five dollars and told him to catch more of them if he could.

CHAPTER 22

Doug was proud of his lynx kitten. It made him a perfect pet but he was afraid somebody would raise cain about him keeping him. He was going to take that chance anyway. Doug never told the banker how he had spared the mama cat and the rest of the family of cats.

He thought if the banker ever found that out, he wouldn't like that worth a hoot. Instead of him trying to keep them, he was supposed to be trying to get rid of them. Doug was proud of his five dollars. Proud that he'd killed ole howler. Proud he'd caught him a pet. Doug named his pet cat Tom Cougar.

The boy had a lot of fun with Tom Cougar and the dogs. The girls like the pet but were a little afraid of him. He didn't cater to them like he did Doug. Tom knew who fed and petted him.

It wasn't long before Tom Cougar could run all the dogs under the floor when he took a notion. He just was about the boss around here. But yet he was a wonderful pet. He didn't bother anything unless it bothered him. He just seemed to get along fine.

Doug wouldn't have taken anything for Tom Cougar. He was a lot of company to him. He would climb all over him and ride his shoulders. He was hoping that none of the neighbors would find out about him having the lynx and make him quit keeping it. He especially didn't want them to tell the banker.

Doug kept expecting Mr. Davis to come by. He always nosed around. Sure enough, one day he heard a horse coming up the little ole dirt road. It was Davis.

He said, "Boy, I hear you got a lot of furs and you're trapping a whole lot. I don't think you've got a hunter's license or a trapper's license."

Doug said, "No sir, I don't."

The law officer said, "Well, I'm gonna have to take your furs in. I oughta take you to jail too, but it'll make it hard on you and that probation you're on. So I'll just take your furs in, as for now."

Doug needed those furs. He maybe had fifty dollars worth in the barn. He thought he might try to buy him a milk cow if he could sell them all at one time. Maybe he'd buy him some better shoes to be out in the weather with. His sisters needed some shoes, too, for going to school.

Doug wanted so much to get enough material for his mother to make her a new dress. Star hadn't had a new one in so long a time.

Mr. Davis goes out and takes a big bag and starts putting one fur of hide in it after the other. Doug had a mink or two, which was worth six or seven dollars a piece back then. He also had a few coon and fox furs and what have you. Yet, the boy didn't have a trapper's license.

Doug watched Davis continue to collect all the furs and then he left. They boy felt so bad. He had worked so hard and spent many lonely hours getting all these pieces together.

About a week later Davis still hadn't turned the furs over to the county seat in Lafayette yet. He happened to be in the bank and spoke to Nash. He laughed and said, "I've got your boy again."

The banker said, "Ah yea, what for Mr. Davis?"

"Well, he's trapping without a license. I went over and picked up his furs and I'm gonna turn them over to the county seat. I didn't take him in yet. I thought I'd talk to you about it and see what you thought."

The banker said, "Mr. Davis, it seems like you got something against that kid and his family. I believe if you'll read your law books or knew anything about the law, you'd know that you're going to have to take those furs back to the kid. He's a juvenile and doesn't have to have a hunting or trapping license. If it wasn't for that, I don't know how the family would survive. He learned all that from his dad, and I'm glad for the family.''

Then he explained, ''Doug really does well with it. Until he becomes of age to have a license, he won't have to have one, and you have gone and taken his furs illegally, you damn dummy!''

Davis raised his voice a little and said, ''Well, I'm still gonna turn them in to the county seat! That boy don't need to be trapping up and catching up all the furs around here anyway! Just cause he's got a high skill at it, cause he's an Indian!''

The banker said, ''I'll just call the judge over at Lafayette and see what he says, and save you a trip. Every one of them furs better be in that bag, too!'' The banker was very upset with the lawman. Nash told Davis that he knew just about how many pieces the boy had too.

So Nash got on the ole crank phone and called two or three operators to get over to the Lafayette courthouse. He got a hold of the judge over there and the judge wanted to know how old the boy was. Nash said, ''Doug is fifteen.''

''Well,'' the judge said, ''you better take them furs back over there to that kid. There ain't nothing we can do about that.''

The banker told Mr. Davis what the judge had said. It looked like he had got another letdown, about as bad as when ole Smut used to mess with his horse and let him get hurt. The ole horse was getting old now, too. Mr. Davis was getting pretty old but it seemed like he still had something against that Indian family.

So Roy loaded the bag of furs on his horse and carried them back to Doug. He just about half apologized to Doug. I reckon his ignorance was the reason he wanted to apologize, to show Doug maybe he was that much of a man.

Doug told him it was okay, but he really did need those furs. He was glad he had them back. He was glad the banker had stepped in there for his cause. The banker didn't trust Davis enough; he thought he might take the furs and try to sell them himself. He figured Doug knew about how many pieces he had.

He'd be sure to check with Doug the next time he saw him to make sure Davis hadn't kept any of them.

Before leaving, Davis happened to see Tom Cougar on top of the house. He said, "Well, how come that lynx is hanging around on your house like that Doug? Aren't you afraid of him?"

Doug said, "No, that don't seem to be a bad one. He just comes around every once in a while. He eats some of the stuff I throw out there." He was trying not to let the grim old man know that he was his own pet. Doug sure was glad Tom Cougar wasn't in his cage.

"Well, why don't you kill him for five dollars and turn him in to the banker?" he questioned.

Doug replied, "Because he's not a bad cat, I don't think."

Thinking of the money and another way to get at the Indian boy one more time Davis said, "Well, I'll just take him in to the banker myself."

He pulled out his gun and Doug shouted, "Stop."

Then Doug told him the story. He said, "I wish you wouldn't do that. He doesn't bother anything and he doesn't bother anybody. I wish you wouldn't bother him." Doug's voice was weak and trembling, he was so mad. Yet he was still at the lawman's mercy.

The lawman said, "Boy, you're still illegal. You know you're not supposed to keep a wild animal here!"

Doug replied, "Mr. Davis, as long as this kitten doesn't bother anybody or anything I want to keep him. If he ever gets unruly or anything, I'll call you and you can have five dollars for him."

Seems like that got to Mr. Davis. He said, "Well, I'll have to go through the banker anyway. If I killed that cat he wouldn't give me five dollars anyway, after you got over there and told him the story. You keep that cat, keep the furs, and I'll leave you alone from now on. Especially, as long as that banker stands behind your back."

So the lawman got on his old horse and rode away and seems like he just left Doug alone for a while. In the meantime,

Janie had gone back to her home again. Doug missed her. He never thought there would ever really be anything between them, but he missed her very much. When he was around the farm, Doug didn't get to spend much time with her, but he missed her presence when she wasn't where he was.

Doug would lie in bed at night and wonder where she was, wishing she was there with him. He seemed to know that some day or another she'd meet some nice young man in school, where she went to school. Then she wouldn't be interested in him anymore. Still Doug looked forward to her coming back to the banker's house in the late summer months. He just couldn't get rid of his thoughts.

When time drew nearer for Janie to return to the farm he would catch himself standing and gazing up the hill at the big house, hoping he could see her again. It was so lonely looking around this big and beautiful home. Mrs. Nash never got out for anything and the banker was always gone. Life was so lonely for Doug. Sometimes he could hardly make it. Some nights he would lie by his window and hear all the sounds of the night while everyone else was supposed to be asleep. Often he would hear his mother weeping, crying and sobbing late at night for the loss of her husband and the hardships that she and her children had.

The sounds of her crying and weeping mixed with all the other night sounds such as the owl and whippoorwill put Doug at the bottom of his small world.

CHAPTER 23

Late one summer, mama Star came down with typhoid fever. She became critically ill in just three days. Doug got the country doctor, Dr. Lee Peterson, who came out to the house and looked at her. Doc Peterson told Doug there wasn't much he could do for her.

A few days later Star was dead. Her death left the three kids alone. It was such a sad time. They put their mama away in the little cemetery with big Jim.

Now the three kids had to make it on their own. Eva Ann was courting a boy at school; she was almost ready to get out of school herself. The boy worked for the sawmill man; his name was Vince Mitchell. Eva, who was now seventeen, finished school and married Vince. It seemed like the death of her mother made her eager to get out of the home. It was so lonely.

This left Doug and Sally Star at home. It was real lonely for Doug, and, of course, for Sally too. Doug carried the load, trying to make things work. He was optimistic that between him and his dogs and Tom Cougar he'd make it.

Tom Cougar got to where he followed Doug around like the dogs. In the forest, he ran and climbed the trees and howled and squawled and almost made the hair raise up on Doug's head and neck. Yet, Doug was glad to have him along. He was a little bit afraid that Tom Cougar would leave him.

The cat had begun to wander and go off and stay a day and night at a time and not come around the house. Doug thought his pet was doing some courting out in the forest at night.

Doug talked to Sap about it one day when he and Cougar were on Jones' place. Mr. Jones was talking about how mean these cats was, but Tom was a beautiful animal with his dark, dark gray hair and gold spot and yellow eyes.

Tom was getting a little age on him now and he and the dogs didn't get along. The dogs pestered him a lot although they never would really take a hold of him. But Tom would often nail them by the nose with one of his claws. Those dogs knew better than to tie into him.

Mr. Jones said, "If you're afraid he's gonna leave you, we can castrate him. It might take a lot of life out of him, but he'll come near to staying home with you. It might stop him from cattin' around so much, ha, ha!" Sap giggled.

"Well," Doug said, "if I knew that would keep him at home I wouldn't mind. He's got to where he howls a lot. He gets on top of the house, especially at nights, just howling. I think he's as lonely as I am. I'm afraid he will leave and not come back, so maybe we'd better castrate him."

Sap didn't know how they were going to hold the big cat down. He said, "Well, if we had him down at the house we've got a little ole tarpaulin that we could wrap him in. If you can hold him, I'll do the work."

So Sap and Doug went off the hill to the barn to get the tarpaulin. Doug got to playing with Tom Cougar and he got him on that ole tarpaulin and threw it up over the cat's back and head.

Then before he knew it, Tom Cougar was balled up in it so Doug could hold him. He was rolled up in there pretty tight so Doug sat down on him. Then Mr. Jones proceeded to castrate him. The little shiner said, "He won't die, but he will think he's going to!"

Oh, he was a sick cat. He just couldn't hardly sit up. He couldn't hardly go. Doug started the journey back through the forest under the large timber home.

Tom Cougar didn't climb any trees that day. He barely kept up with Doug and the dogs. Doug got him home and fed him good. Tom Cougar went to the barn, climbed up and lay in a little bit of hay that was in there. He just lay around for about a week. It was pitiful.

Doug was almost afraid he was going to die. But Tom Cougar finally came out of this situation. He just seemed to keep growing and getting bigger and fatter and more beautiful all the time.

Doug went on working for the banker, a little in the bank, but mostly in the barn and around the farm, breaking horses. He was an extra good rider. Doug wasn't afraid of horses, even though he had seen one break his dad's neck.

The banker was well pleased the way he broke the stock for him. Doug just kept the good thing going. The banker could sell them for a right smart more money when they were broke, plus he'd give Doug a little extra of the profit, not much, but some.

One day the banker said, "Boy, there's going to be a fair in Lafayette, Tennessee. From what I see in them mules of yours, they might be good in two classes."

Doug said, "What do you mean I could do good in two classes?"

"Well, the mules pull good don't they?"

"Yes."

"The banker went on, "We'll take some of my best harnesses and tassels and brass knobs and dress them up. They might even do good in the show ring. Then we can put them in the pulling contest if you want to."

Doug said, "It's a long way to go and get back in one night."

Then Nash said, "Well, we'll leave here about one o'clock in the afternoon and make a pleasure trip out of it. Janie is coming back, and we'll get her and your sisters and your brother-in-law to go too. We can all go. Ya'll can all go on the wagon, and I'll go in the buggy. We'll go up to that fair and see how you'll do."

Doug smiled and said, "O.K."

The kid was jumpin' for joy inside, thinking that the banker was that interested in his mules and that they might be that good.

But the real joy was that Janie was coming back soon and could go with them. Doug would be able to show off his mules.

CHAPTER 24

Time came for the fair. Doug curried and brushed up his mules and sheared them and shoed them. Those mules were looking good and doing good. Doug dressed them up in two fine harnesses then hooked them to the wagon.

After putting a little hay on the wagon, he got Eva Ann, Janie Sally Star and Vince together and they all took off about one o'clock to go to Lafayette. Everyone was bubbling over with joy and having fun. It was a business trip and a hay ride all in one.

Of course, Janie sat up front with Doug. The banker trailed along behind them in the buggy like a chaperon. Still he was a little bit jealous of his granddaughter and the Indian boy, even though he knew she couldn't beat the boy.

The banker also wanted to go to the fair to see how them mules would do. He thought maybe he had a little to do with it since he had given Doug the old mare. Janie thought maybe her grandfather had had a change of heart; at least she was hoping so.

They arrived in Lafayette and Doug entered his mules in the show ring. He came up with a second blue ribbon. Doug was tickled pink about it. A lot of good stock was there, to be sure, and he came in second place.

He never thought he would own anything that near to perfect. They were all very pleased for Doug, even the banker. Next was the mule pulling contest. Doug decided to enter in that. Course, Janie and his sisters were sitting on the sidelines watching and cheering him on. Looked like his mules didn't do as well as they would out in the woods or on the farm. But anyhow, Doug didn't have a chance against some of those mules that were trained for such occasions.

Even though he wasn't good in the pull, he was still tickled pink with his second class ribbon. Just so happened, a man named Harry Carson wanted to know if Doug would sell that pair of mules.

Doug told him, No, he didn't reckon that he would. He needed the money out of them, but you don't find many twin teams of mules.

Carson said, "You mean these mules are twins?"

Doug replied, "Yeah, twins, belong to one mother and born on the same day."

Then Carson seemed to get a little more itchy for them. "Would you price them mules to me?"

Doug said, "Well, they would be too high. I really don't want to sell them, but I really could use the money." Doug finally said he'd take a hundred and fifty dollars for them.

Carson wanted to know if the harness was included. Doug explained that it wasn't his harness. Well, this guy wouldn't give that kind of money for them right now, but he would sure like to have them.

After that everybody loaded up and went back home. Doug was still surprised and tickled about his ribbon. He carried the wagon back home and put up the banker's harness. Then he headed on home with his mules, still thinking about Janie, and how beautiful she was. He sure was glad to see her again. Seemed like she got more beautiful and more mature all the time. Yet Doug knew the banker was still set against them spending time together alone.

Maybe it was because she was his only granddaughter. The banker might even be jealous of her with any guy, Doug thought. Anyhow, he figured the banker would step in if anything started to happen between them. Doug couldn't help the way the banker thought, anymore that he could help being half Indian.

One evening Doug was over to feed early, and of course, Janie was up walking around in the yard. She had a little stick, and was twirling it this, that and the other way. Doug was out behind the barn and could see a young foal up in the holler at a distance. He had to go up and see about it.

Janie climbed the fence. She was going to go with him. The banker had gotten in early that same evening, but the kids didn't know it. The two headed up towards the new foal holding hands.

That was something new for them. Both of their hearts were beating about like bells. The banker watched them walk up the ravine to the foal. It seemed to be fine. After Doug helped it get up, the foal went over to its mother and started nursing. Janie was thrilled as she watched the baby staggering and wobbling around trying to get its head under the mama to get a tit.

Doug and Janie turned and started back down the holler, still holding hands while the banker watched from the house. Not knowing the banker had come home, Doug and Janie walked towards the barn.

Janie just stood there. She didn't have much to talk about either. Finally, at last, they embraced and kissed as the banker watched.

Suddenly he hollered, "Janie, you better come on to the house!"

This sacred Janie because she thought he might be raw about it. She went to the house and the banker came down to the barn.

He said, "Boy, you are taking too much advantage. You're putting yourself in jeopardy. I won't tolerate you seeing my granddaughter like this! No telling how long you've been slipping around like this."

Doug said, "Well, I'm very sorry, Mr. Nash, if that's the way you feel. I'll try to avoid her. I don't know how it all came about, but I'll try to avoid her if that's the way you feel, because I do need my job."

The banker replied, "No, Doug, you don't have a job anymore! You're through here! To think you might go behind my back and do things like that. Just don't come back around anymore. I'll make it some way without you."

Doug said, "Sure. But Mr. Nash, if and when you get to a better world, and there are some Indians there, where will you sit?"

These words from Doug really stunned the banker, but he didn't say a thing. Doug went home and got to thinking that the banker would probably foreclose his loan. He owed three hundred more dollars on his little ole farm.

Doug decided he would try to get in touch with that guy, Carson, and sell him the mules.

So one day Doug went across the creek to a neighbor who owned one of those crank-type telephones which were the only kind they had in those days. He hated to sell his mules and felt blue. And he also hated to think of the banker objecting so much to him and Janie. It really wasn't his fault, anyway, Doug told himself. He couldn't help loving the girl. He didn't think she could help loving him either.

Janie was pretty as she could be. To her Doug was right handsome. He was just really down on his luck. She knew his world had tumbled and she was sorry. She knew she was the cause.

Just then Doug heard a horse coming up the road. He looked up and saw a big white horse carrying a mount. The mount was Carson.

The man rode up to Doug and said, "Hello, how are you doing? Have you still got your mules?"

"Yeah."

"Are you going to keep them?"

Doug answered, "Well, I'd like to." He was trying not to let on that he was eager to sell his mules.

Then Carson said, "Well, I came here to stay a day or two, to take some baths and drink some of the water. I heard you lived around here close and I inquired about you. I thought I'd look you up and see if I might still buy them mules, if you'd sell them."

Doug then explained that he didn't much believe he wanted to sell them. He didn't want the man to know it, but he was ready to sell his mules.

Carson spoke up again, "Well, I'll tell you, I'll give you the hundred and fifty dollars you want, even if the harness doesn't come with them."

Doug paused and thought a minute to himself. As bad as he hated to, deep down he knew he had to do it. So Doug finally said, "Okay, I'll let you buy them."

Doug took the hundred and fifty dollars to the bank to pay Mr. Nash. Nash was a little bit unfriendly. He told the boy he appreciated his paying, but he'd have to have the rest of it before long.

Doug was up a tree on that. He didn't have any way of getting the rest of the money at that time. He had sold the fifty dollars worth of furs in the fall, before his mother died and bought an old cow to get milk and butter from. Doug didn't want to have to sell her too.

There was nobody at the house but Doug and Sally Star. She wasn't the best cook, but, at least she could bake bread. The two would eat milk and bread and butter a lot of times.

They had other things to eat though. Doug had learned a little about cooking meat from his dad. Doug didn't want to sell the ole cow. He probably couldn't get much for her anyway. Of course, he had to take part of the fifty dollars to put his mother away.

Now that Eva Ann had moved out it didn't seem like much of a home, especially since Doug couldn't see Janie anymore and didn't have a job.

CHAPTER 25

One evening Doug decided he would walk across the woods and talk to Mr. Jones. Ole Sap was getting pretty old and feeble. He got over there and looked around and didn't hear or see Sap on the farm, anywhere. Doug went on down to the house and found Sap and Sally sitting on the porch.

Both of them looked very frail and old. Seemed like they were glad to see Doug come in. He was like a grandchild to them. Both of them tried to talk to him at the same time, asking how he and the girls were doing. What they had been up to? They also asked about the mules and Tom Cougar.

Doug sat down and told the old couple he had sold the mules to pay on his little farm so he could keep it. And about the banker taking his job away from him, and running him off on account of Janie. They sympathized with him.

Mrs. Jones said to Sap, "We got no kids and we're getting old; we've got money we won't ever need. Let this boy have that other hundred and fifty dollars to pay the banker."

Sap even had that much cash in his pocket. Guess he'd been selling a little bit of that ole shine. Sap reached into his pocket and pulled out a hundred dollar bill and then a fifty dollar bill. He handed both bills to Doug and said, "Boy, this will heal Joe's pain and yours."

Doug told him he didn't know how he could ever pay it back or when he could ever pay it back. Sap grinned. Then with a big lump in his throat and a shaky voice, he said, "Well, there'll be nobody to fret about it, if you don't ever. But if you do, then

133

fine. Seems like what we've got will have to be left to charity anyway. You might as well be part of the charity.''

Doug assured them he didn't want it that way. He would go and do the best he could do. If he could ever get another job when he got older, he would try to repay them one way or another.

The old couple didn't seem to be worried about it. Doug felt deep down in his heart that these people were his true friends and knew that they loved him. It done him good. He thanked them and went on back across the big forest, just wandering around admiring mother nature's beauty and listening to her sweet songs, and feeling a little better.

Doug got on back home to Sally Star and found her sitting there crying. He tried to find out what she was crying about. She was now a little over fourteen years old. Sally Star told Doug she was in love with a guy who came around the school when he wasn't working; he was already out of school. Doug couldn't believe it.

Sally Star hated to leave him, but she and this guy, Samuel Doss had planned to get married even as young as she was. Doug said, ''Well, if that's the way it is, that's the way it is. You want him and he wants you. I wouldn't want to stand in the way, because it seems like we don't get much happiness like it is.''

Then Sally Star told Doug, ''We're getting married as soon as school is out this time.''

Doug replied, ''Fine and dandy.'' He was pleased for the kid. She was too young to get married, but was so lonely. She spent much of her time alone, for Doug was gone most of the time.

Time went on but Doug wasn't in a hurry to pay the banker his other hundred and fifty dollars. School finally was out and Sally Star got married. Now Doug was all alone.

By this time, Jip had gotten old and crippled. She wasn't much good, but at least Doug still had Rascal, Gypsy and Tom Cougar. It was real lonely now around the place. Seemed like he'd lost his whole family in just a few years. He didn't have a job, but Doug could live in the woods by himself, if he had to.

One day Doug decided to give the banker his hundred and fifty dollars. He went up to one of the cashiers to pay his money and get his note.

Nash saw him and dropped what he was doing, "Hello, young man. What are you doing, boy?"

Doug replied, "I'm paying off my note. I'm afraid you might foreclose on me and take the little ole farm back. Then I wouldn't have anywhere to live. At least, I do have somewhere to live! And since I don't have to have anybody depending on me, I can make it now."

The banker said, "I don't want your money. I assure you I won't foreclose. I'll tell you what I want, boy."

"I hope you don't want no more burning done. I can get by without anything like that and you too!"

Then the banker said, "I want you to work out the rest of the money with me. I need you back. I really need you down on the farm again. That guy I got down there, he couldn't break any horses. He's afraid of the stable stock."

He went on pleading and said, "Doug, boy, I need you back, and I want to apologize for being so rude and mean about you and Janie."

Doug felt good to think maybe he had changed Nash's mind, but he would still like to have stomped the stuff out of him for it all!

Of course at that time, Janie had gone back to Georgia. Doug reconsidered. Then he said, "No, I believe I'll let you take this money. This is the law and I want to pay my note."

Nash begged, "Doug don't make me take it. We can work something out later, maybe a better deal?"

"You must take it!" the boy said.

Deep down Doug was pretty hurt. He almost couldn't accept the apology. He didn't think Janie would ever come back and spend the summer with her grandparents; plus she was older and she was hurt as well.

Doug thought he might reconsider working for the banker. But he'd have to think about it. After all, he didn't have a job or any way to get by other than by living off the land. But he did get his note. Then he burned it up, and now he owned the little ole farm. He had it looking good, yet there wasn't much future there, just one guy living by himself, with no job. But he could make his kind of living without the banker.

So he told the banker he'd let him know in a few days whether he'd come back to work for him or not. The memory he had of Janie would not go away night or day. It was so sweet in his mind. He thought if this is love, it was sweet as well as bitter. In some ways it hurt so bad.

CHAPTER 26

Doug was so lonesome and empty with nothing to do, a few days later he decided to go over and take the banker up on his offer. He believed that the banker had changed his mind, and that when Janie came back, if she ever did, things would be different.

Somehow Doug felt like something good was going to happen. He longed so much for her to return. So Doug went over to the bank and asked for Mr. Nash. He was in the back. Nash heard Doug out front and told him to come on in.

Doug went in, and again Mr. Nash apologized to him. He told him how glad he was that his two sisters had apparently married a couple of very good guys. Even though they were half Indian, he was proud of them and him for settling down in the neighborhood.

Doug still seemed to be at a loss for words. Finally, he spoke up and told the banker he would come back to work for him till he could find something else to do. He'd break horses and mend harnesses and things like he'd been doing before.

But Doug explained that he didn't care to work at the bank anymore. That wasn't really his type of work. He'd rather have a full time job just for farm work and helping the tenants.

Nash told him if that's what he wanted, it was okay with him. But he still wished he'd work in the bank some too. The banker said, ''It's good for your education. What little you got, it seems to be good, and it would be good for you.''

Doug said, ''Well, I'll just work a little while like it is. I might consider working at the bank later.'' He felt like he could be more independent now that he didn't owe the bank anymore.

Doug worked on the farm for Nash, but he'd be at home at night so lonely. He'd hear the dogs out there when it wasn't hunting time, yet it seemed like something was out in the woods waiting.

Tom Cougar climbed the porch post and got on the boards. Doug could hear his claws. It seemed like he was tearing the boards off. Tom howled and squawled in the woods at night and sounded so lonely. Doug still thought how unfortunate life seemed to be for him, compared with some boys he knew.

But one way or another Doug thought everything would work out. He loved to hear that old cat howl. Since he had the doors shut and the windows down, it did sound a little bougery.

Doug would lie in bed at night sleepless and start thinking of Janie wondering when she'd come back, or if she would ever come back. Would she care about him when she came back? He kept thinking how pretty she was for the other boys at school to look at and how they must like to talk to her.

The banker was feeling very, very guilty. He also lay in bed thinking and arguing with himself. He'd say, "Well, I don't blame Janie for caring about the boy. He's very intelligent, he's big and husky, and he's handsome."

Then he'd turn right around and say, "I don't blame the boy for caring about Janie. She's a fine girl, a beautiful girl. So I guess I've got in the middle of something."

He thought, "I should have just stayed out of it. What they do about it from now on is their business. I'll try to leave it alone."

Sure enough, the next year when school was out, Janie came to her grandfather's farm to spend a month or two as usual. She had always enjoyed being on the farm but this time she didn't think she would since her grandfather had taken over and been so rude to her. He even told her once that he would stop her from coming to the farm if she didn't quit seeing Doug.

Janie didn't have anything to do at home where she lived. She loved to be out in the country. Janie was pretty much a tomboy anyway. When she got back to the farm she didn't know Doug had started back to work for the banker.

One day she was out in back of the house just gandering at the sky and the surroundings. Then she happened to look down towards the barn and saw a guy. He sure looked like Doug.

She thought, it can't be. Not after the way he and grandpa talked. He never would be down at the barn again. Surely it wasn't Doug, she thought. But her heart was pounding at the thought, just hoping. What if it is Doug? she smiled.

Doug looked up at her thinking she wouldn't have anything to do with him. Still he decided he'd just see if she would speak to him. He waved and called out, "Hello there!"

She said, "Is that you, Doug?"

Doug spoke again, "Yes, it is."

Then Janie went running towards him, almost jumping the fence in her hurry. "I don't care what grandpa says, I love you, I love you!" By then she was almost in tears.

Doug said, "Well, maybe it ain't as bad as you think. Your grandfather has reconsidered, I think. He asked me to come back to work for him even though I paid off my little farm note. But I still owe Mr. Jones for it. I thought I'd rather owe Sap and show him I'm ambitious. I can pay him the same as I can pay the banker with the money I work out from him. But I don't think he's that bad now."

He went on to say, "I really think he's sorry the way he acted and maybe things will be better from now on."

That tickled Janie very much. She hadn't even heard that Doug was back working for the banker.

About that time Nash pulled up in front of the barn lot and called to them. He seemed to be very pleased that the kids were together. He told Doug to take ole Bet, unharness her, put her up and feed her. So Doug and Janie walked through the horses across the pastures.

Seemed like the old man had broken through to where he could see the light. Money wasn't everything. He only had one granddaughter; why would he want to make her unhappy?

Doug and Janie came back to the barn and Doug went home to do his chores. Janie and her grandfather went to the house and the old man asked her about marriage.

Janie replied, "If he loves me as much as I love him, then someday we'll probably get married, whether you do or don't like it, although we would be obliged if you would condone it, and wish us happiness.

The old man had tears in his eyes and said with a trembling voice, "That's what I wish."

Janie was so surprised. She grabbed him around the neck and hugged him and told him she loved him, and that she appreciated his feeling that way.

The banker said, "Well, I guess I'm a spoiled, jealous old man. I sit at the bank and listen to people's problems. I don't really get time to get out and know what life is all about or to enjoy it."

Janie asked, Why did you bring up the subject of marriage? Doug hasn't brought it up, yet."

The old man smiled and said, "Well, from what I see, I think he'll bring it up before long." The old man was bubbling over with joy because he had finally accepted the situation.

Janie grinned and said, "Well, I hope so."

It wasn't long till Janie was back down by the barn lot again where Doug was working with the horses. She was watching him breaking horses and riding them. Finally, he asked her, "Ever ride a horse?"

Janie said, "I've always wanted to, but I don't want to ride the kind you're riding, I don't see how you can stay on them wild critters, they are so mean and ornery."

"Well, we got some others to ride and it's just like sitting in a swing. If you want to ride, I'll put a saddle on one of them." Doug said.

Then Janie smiled and said, "Saddle 'em up, I'd like to take a ride."

Doug saddled up a strawberry roan mare. It was a real saddle horse. He put his saddle on a better horse than those young bucking things up there he was fooling with. The two decided they'd take an evening ride over the pastures down by the fences and look at the horses. Doug seemed to be bubbling over in his heart. He was very happy.

Seemed like something he really thought he'd never dream of was about to happen. He thought how bitter life had been for him and now it was so wonderful and sweet. His mind and his eyes wandered up to the blue sky and he thought, Look, mom and dad, I'm okay.

Doug and Janie slowly rode around looking at all the beauty of the country and enjoying each other's presence. Janie reined her horse over against Doug's horse and they stopped. Janie said, "I love this. I love this place, and I love you best of all."

Doug's heart was pounding so hard he could hardly keep it in his body. He finally said, "I love you," and then he kissed her.

Then Doug said, "Have you ever thought about marrying me?" Janie's heart almost jumped out of her mouth. Her face blushed as tears poured off her cheeks.

She said, "Very often; grandpa and I talked about it."

Doug said, "Well, I've had it on my mind. I love you that well, but I really didn't want to ask you to come down to my level, knowing that I'm half Indian, and that your grandfather didn't partake of it so good. I had wanted to ask you, but I didn't want to ask you to bring yourself to where I might be." Doug was so humble.

She said, "Doug, I'll marry you anytime you want to. I think grandfather wants us to get married." Then she said, "We must go, it's getting late."

Janie reined her horse away and kicked her in the sides and said, "I bet you can't catch me."

Suddenly she went down the hillside in a hard run. The mare fell and Janie went tumbling across the rocky ground and just lay there all sprawled out and totally breathless. Her dress was up around her waist and her legs were bare; Doug thought they were beautiful.

He jumped off his horse and went to her. She wasn't breathing. She had a bloody spot on her head. He felt her face and hands and they seemed to be holding their warmth.

So Doug turned her over on her face and got to pumping her ribs up and down. Then Janie heaved and started breathing. Doug was so relieved. He knew she had a chance. Maybe she wasn't hurt too bad. She heaved a few more deep breaths and turned over and looked up at Doug and said, "Oh, my head hurts."

"No wonder, you must have hit a rock when you fell off that mare. That's a pretty nasty, bump on your head. But I don't think it's too serious. Just got the wind knocked out of you, more or less, I think."

Janie's head and neck hurt a lot. She was in so much pain she could hardly keep from crying, but she didn't want Doug to know.

She said, "Yes, silly me, anyway, trying to ride fast the first time I was ever on a horse. I was so happy I wanted to show off. It was right silly of me wasn't it."

Doug picked her up and said, "I shouldn't have let you ride a horse by yourself for the first time. The mare is okay, I think, but she thought you wanted her to run. So that's what she did.

Janie said, "I'll be okay, a little sore, but okay. Like you said, I think it just knocked the wind out of me, and a little bit of the other stuff too, Ha ha!"

Her horse had run on back to the barn so Doug got her up in his saddle then climbed up behind her. He didn't mind that at all. It was a good chance to keep his arms around Janie a little longer. She fit very well in his arms. He didn't think the little wound on her head was going to amount to much. Doug felt something coming over his body. He believed it was waves of love.

They finally got back to the barn and caught the mare and put the horses up. Doug said, "By the way, if we are going to marry, when did you have in mind? Do you think you could live in that little house across the creek over yonder and be satisfied? It's not big but it's sturdy and comfortable and there's cold spring water running at the edge of the yard.

Janie smiled and said, "The house is fine. Whenever you want to get married is fine, too."

Doug said, "Well, let me think it over. I'll have to try to get a little money together to get a marriage license, and to pay a preacher."

She said, "Take your time, it's fine with me."

Doug asked, "By the way, why don't you come over and see the little house. You haven't ever seen my little kitten over there. The banker doesn't even know I've got it. He might be a little raw if he knew I had that kitten."

Janie was curious to know what he was talking about a kitten, and why would the banker care about a cat?

He grinned and said, "Just wait til you come and I'll show you. His name is Tom Cougar. He's the best pet I ever had."

Janie replied, "Well, sometime when you are over, and grandpa isn't using Ole Bet and the buggy, we'll just hook up and drive over."

Doug said, "That'll be fine with me."

There was a watering trough beside the barn, so Janie knelt down and washed the blood off her face. Then she went up to the house and told her grandparents about her wreck. She also told them she would be marrying Doug in a little while. They both seemed to be very happy for her.

Ma Nell checked the big bump on her head and they told her it would go away in a few days. They were just glad she wasn't badly hurt. Now she had fallen off a horse and in love.

CHAPTER 27

A few days later, Doug took Janie over to the little ole farm and the little home. She thought she'd like it all, maybe because she loved Doug so much. She thought anything or anywhere would be right for both of them.

Both the dogs came running out to meet them when they drove up. Tom Cougar wasn't around to be seen. Janie asked Doug about it. She said, "Where's this kitten you were telling me about?"

Doug replied, "He'll be around after a while, I guess?" The two of them walked around a little while, looking around and hollering for Tom Cougar.

Directly she saw the big, dark-gray cat with yellow dots all over him, coming at her. It scared her.

Doug held out his arms and Cougar jumped into them. Cougar was a big cat now, and just about as big as "ole howler" was. When Janie realized the cat was just a pet, she fell in love with him and patted him and rubbed him behind his ears. He purred just like any ole house cat would.

Janie saw right away that she was going to like that kitten. She didn't press her luck though; if he didn't like her, he could be dangerous. She gave herself time to get acquainted with him.

Doug and Janie talked about the future and how hard it would be to get by. Doug didn't have much of a job and still owed Mr. Jones a hundred and fifty dollars. Janie didn't seem to mind.

So they made their plans to get married before too long. Doug finally got enough money ahead to buy a few groceries and get the marriage license and give a little to the preacher.

One glorious day in August, Doug got their license. He hitched up a work horse to an old buggy and they went to town and found a justice of the peace and got married. The ceremony was short but sweet. Doug and Janie were both just gleaming all over. Eva Ann and Sally Star were there with their husbands. The two sisters stood up with Janie as her bridesmaids and Sap stood beside Doug as his best man.

Janie's dress was just lovely. She and her grandma had made an ivory dress with lace trim and pearl buttons. Doug thought she was the most beautiful thing in Macon County, as they stood side by side on that summer day and said their vows.

After the wedding they all gathered at Nash's house for a celebration. Ma Nell had baked a delicious pineapple cream cake and they had homemade fruit punch which was served in the family heirloom crystal goblets.

Everyone was well pleased with the way things were going, with the marriage and all. Doug was a little shy eating up there. He thought maybe he was getting a little above his raising. But the old man was pleased with his grandson. He chuckled and told him, ''Well, I only have one granddaughter, now I only got one grandson.'' He made them feel like he was proud of both of them. After the party was over Doug and Janie walked across the creek in the dark over to the little dream house which became their honeymoon suite.

Anyway, things went along just fine. On rainy nights that ole cat would get on top of the house. Doug and Janie could hear his toenails. They sounded as if they were peeling the boards loose. Tom would do a lot of howling on rainy nights; he seemed to be more lonely. His voice would sound deeper and a little more spooky.

Doug liked that because when the ole cat howled, Janie crawled up a little closer to him. They enjoyed their lives and didn't worry about acquiring wealth.

CHAPTER 28

One day Doug and Janie were over in the little boom town and went up to the bank to see Grandpa Nash. He seemed to be very pleased they had come to visit the bank. They suspected he'd been sippin Mr. Jones tonic. Anyway, he was very relaxed.

He called them back in his office and said, "Well, boy, I've got one more favor to ask of you."

Doug smiled and said, "As long as it's not burning another ole hotel or something like that."

The banker chuckled and said, "I'm sorry about that boy, but this favor is a bit more in your favor."

Doug said, "Well, let's have it. What is it?"

The banker continued, "Well, I need a secretary and a vice president for this bank, and I think my two grandchildren will fit the bill. You don't have to have a lot of education to be vice president, or president either. You just tell people what to do. I need a vice president and we could always use a secretary or teller, or what have you. I wonder if you would do me that favor and take the job?"

Doug said, "Well, that's esteeming me pretty high, but with your help around here, I guess we can manage it, if it's allright with Janie."

Janie agreed and said it would be fine with her. That way they'd all be right there together. It would give Doug a good opportunity and maybe someday he'd be president of the bank. They were a happy little family all together.

The short, bald-headed man had a great feeling of satisfaction deep down inside; now he would prove his love for the kids.

The little ole place over there held many memories for Doug; how he had strived to get by and feed his sisters and mother; how he had to give up Gris. How he could have died like Gris.

It held a lot of memories, but all the memories he would have there from now on would be pleasurable. Everything went fine for him and Janie from then on.

Doug wouldn't have taken a penny for that ole cat. Janie liked the cat too. Doug always loved to hear that ole cat climbing the post to get up on the boards. He'd never forget his childhood memories because he missed his mother and sisters, but Doug was very, very happy now. Seemed like everything was going to be plumb allright for the Child of the Depression.

As far as any one could see, he would be running the big farm and the bank too. Doug would always love Janie and the little town of many waters.

I myself can almost hear that ole tom cat on that house, clawing at the boards and howling in his loneliness. I, too, have spent a lot of lonely hours like that. Seems like sometimes the sounds of nature were just music to my ears. Just like I've heard a few ole owls out when I was alone. It seemed like they were telling me something, like everything's okay.

. . .So, that's the way this little story ends. I hope somebody enjoyed part of it. Thank you for reading.

P.S. Don't ever give up your dream!

.